Trac

D0985637

A Candlelight
Ecstasy Classic Romance

"SIMON, NO! PLEASE LET ME GO!" SHE BEGGED.

"Don't ask me to stop, Kirsten," he whispered in a low, husky voice. "I want you so badly . . ."

"You want me!" she screamed, pulling back from him. "That's supposed to be enough, is it? The fact that you want me? Well, it isn't! Not nearly enough!"

Simon lifted his head to gaze down into her angry face. "Why are you so afraid? I promise I'll make you want me, too. It won't be all one-sided, honey. You can relax and enjoy the relationship. I would never hurt you."

"Don't talk to me about 'relationships'! I'm not in the mood for the kind of relationship you have in mind and I never will be!"

Be sure to read this month's other
CANDLELIGHT ECSTASY CLASSIC ROMANCE . . .

THE TAWNY GOLD MAN, *Amii Lorin*

Next month in the
CANDLELIGHT ECSTASY CLASSIC ROMANCE
publishing program, don't miss . . .

THE PASSIONATE TOUCH, *Bonnie Drake*
ONLY THE PRESENT, *Noelle Berry McCue*

CANDLELIGHT ECSTASY ROMANCES®

GENTLE PIRATE

Jayne Castle

A CANDLELIGHT ECSTASY CLASSIC ROMANCE

A CANDLELIGHT ECSTASY CLASSIC ROMANCE
Published by
Dell Publishing Co., Inc.
1 Dag Hammarskjold Plaza
New York, New York 10017

Dell ® TM 681510, Dell Publishing Co., Inc.

A Candlelight Ecstasy Classic Romance

Candlelight Ecstasy Romance®, 1,203,540, is a registered trademark of Dell Publishing Co., Inc., New York, New York.

ISBN: 0-440-12981-8

Printed in the United States of America

One Previous Edition

August 1986

10 9 8 7 6 5 4 3 2 1

WFH

To Our Reader:

By popular demand we are happy to announce that we will be bringing you two Candlelight Ecstasy Classic Romances every month.

In the upcoming months your favorite authors and their earlier best-selling Candlelight Ecstasy Romances® will be available once again.

As always, we will continue to present the distinctive sensuous love stories that you have come to expect only from Ecstasy and also the very finest work from new authors of contemporary romantic fiction.

Your suggestions and comments are always welcome. Please write to us at the address below.

Sincerely,

The Editors
Candlelight Romances
1 Dag Hammarskjold Plaza
New York, New York 10017

CHAPTER ONE

The hard silence in the room was intimidating. It was meant to be. A great many people would have willingly accused Simon Kendrick of many things, Kirsten Mallory suspected, and among those accusations would be the fact that the man was well aware of the effect he created. And, she thought grimly, exerting considerable control over her nervous system to avoid recrossing her legs, he had no compunction about using his ability to intimidate. Any other new manager about to conduct a discussion with an employee would have made at least a few token efforts toward creating a relaxed, friendly atmosphere. Not Simon Kendrick. He continued to appear buried in the paperwork in front of him while Kirsten sat waiting patiently in the plush visitor's chair.

Next time, she decided, she would bring her own paperwork. Or a magazine. It would give her something to do while she awaited his attention. But perhaps those of Mr. Kendrick's subjects who had been summoned to a royal audience weren't supposed to occupy their time until the liege lord was free. It might spoil the calculated effort to put them into the proper humble mood. The thought curved her soft, well-defined lips into a smile and she hastily directed her glance toward the window in case the big man happened to look up and see the barely suppressed amusement. She had a feeling life could get

7

quite miserable in a hurry if he thought she was laughing at him.

"I'll be with you in a moment, Miss Mallory," Kendrick said suddenly.

Kirsten withdrew her glance from the uninviting desert vista visible through the window and returned it to the man sitting behind the huge, littered desk. But he hadn't even changed the focus of his gaze when he had spoken. He hadn't needed to, Kirsten decided. Some instinct must have told him that it was time to give the reins a small tug and she had to admit the deep, rough voice with its easy power was adequate for the task. Against her will, she found herself concentrating on him again instead of the view. With a sense of irritation she watched as he continued rapidly scanning the thick document in front of him, flipping pages frequently with his right hand.

The annoyance she was experiencing, Kirsten knew, was generated as much by her reactions to this man as it was by the man himself. Taking a firm grip on her emotions, she settled back into the soft red chair (done in the color of the company's logo) with determination. No man was going to intimidate her ever again. She had made that vow less than three months ago and Simon Kendrick was not going to make her forget it. All right. If he wanted her attention, he would get it. With a vengeance. Why should she bother to worry about rudeness? It obviously didn't bother him to treat her in that fashion. Kirsten decided that the way to deal with the incipient feelings of intimidation was to analyze what it was about the man that threatened her.

Deliberately she studied the dark, inclined head, noticing with detachment that the hair was cut a little too short to be fashionable. The color was a deep, rich brown and she had the impression that bright sunlight would bring out hints of red. So what? Kirsten asked herself with an inner smile. Brown hair was not particularly intimidating. Her own was brown, for that matter, although a softer, lighter shade. Unfortunately it didn't have deep red highlights, she thought wryly. It was, she knew, that rather nondescript brown that people who are trying to be kind will tell you has blond tones. Kirsten had looked for those

8

blond tones in the mirror several times in her younger days, but at the age of twenty-eight she had finally given up the project. Now, as was her custom during working hours, the long length of it, which reached nearly to her waist, was clipped into a neat coil at the back of her head.

Kirsten continued with her survey, dismissing the danger of Simon Kendrick's hair with a small, silent chuckle. Thick eyebrows shielded eyes of an as yet unknown color. Her own gray pair moved steadily on with the assessment. The face wasn't handsome. The man was somewhere in his late thirties and showed it. The lean, harsh planes of his features caused her to wonder if he ever smiled with genuine warmth, and she decided he probably didn't. The clothes suited the man well, she noted. The crisp white shirt, formal tie, and neatly cut coat echoed the somewhat unfashionable hairstyle. He was a tall, very tall, solidly built man who would have looked vaguely ridiculous dressed in a less conservative fashion. Kirsten tried to picture him in a brightly patterned shirt and failed. She concentrated for a moment on his sheer size, obvious even when he was seated, and decided that was a major intimidating factor. She didn't like men who towered over her. After Jim she knew she would go out of her way to avoid such men.

Kirsten finished her perusal with a quick glance at the strong, square right hand with its rather thick wrist, remembering that office gossip said his left ended in a metal hook. Until now he had kept it out of sight behind the desk. No doubt about it, such a device would add a devastatingly heavy weight on the intimidation side of the scale. Kirsten wondered how he had lost his hand and knew she would never bring herself to ask. No one would ask this man anything personal unless invited to do so! She groaned inwardly, thinking about the prospect of working for this creature for the next several months. It was a cinch he wouldn't know the first thing about libraries. She would have to waste countless hours educating him!

"If you've quite finished dissecting me, we may as well get on with this meeting," Kendrick said unexpectedly, managing to glance up and neatly snag Kirsten's gaze before she could shift it to something, anything else. And now she had the answer to the question about his eyes. They were hazel. Which didn't begin to describe them at all, she thought with a tiny sigh. Hazel eyes were able to reflect the whole range of human emotions and the cold, calculating, almost-green depths of Simon Kendrick's eyes definitely had to be listed as another intimidating factor about the man. Anyone who could project that degree of harsh dominance held a powerful weapon. So chalk one up for the eyes, Kirsten decided. Forewarned is forearmed, and she gathered her own not inconsiderable self-confidence about her like a cloak. The need to speak, to make some sort of comment that would restore this little interview to a more equal footing, drove her into rash words.

"Forgive me, Mr. Kendrick, if I appeared to be staring." She smiled sweetly, trying to imply that she could care less if he really did forgive her. "But I got tired of looking out at Rattlesnake Mountain and you're the next . . ." Kirsten broke off, absolutely horrified at how her tongue had gotten out of control!

"And I was the next largest object around?" He smiled thinly, sparing a brief glance out the window to the huge treeless lump of a mountain known locally as "Rattlesnake." The smile, which barely moved his firm mouth, never reached his eyes. His smiles probably never did.

Kirsten felt herself going quite red and was more than a little surprised. After all, at her age, and after having been made a widow within two months of marriage, she didn't think too many situations could make her lose her poise.

Deciding this was a clear instance of discretion being the better part of valor, she refused to be drawn into a reply she would probably regret. Contenting herself with an apologetic smile, she waited with hidden impatience for the discussions to continue.

He must have reached the conclusion that he had better things to do than bait one of Silco's employees, because after a fractional hesitation Kendrick plunged into the reason why Kirsten had been called to his office.

"As you're well aware, I have only been here for a week, Miss Mallory," he began. "Nevertheless, I think

10

that's long enough to begin asking a few questions. You must have heard that Silco hired me in an effort to trim some of the fat from the organization?"

Kirsten nodded aloofly, thinking she knew now what was coming. Oh, well, it hadn't been a bad job while it lasted. Too bad she hadn't worked long enough to collect unemployment insurance while she hunted another position, but there was enough in the bank to survive. And she didn't really care for Richland, Washington, or electronics firms anyway!

"Few companies as small as Silco maintain reference libraries, as I'm sure you know," he went on calmly, just as if he weren't about to throw her out onto the street. That conjured up a funny image and Kirsten had to struggle to restrain a smile. The thought of this huge man beginning his cost-trimming exercise by hoisting her own one hundred and eight pounds and tossing her out on George Washington Way, the main thoroughfare through town, struck her as humorous. She even had a picture of the expression on Liz Wilford's face as Kendrick carted the librarian past the receptionist's desk! The sleek cat eyes would be gleaming.

"Furthermore," Kendrick continued, "Silco already has a central filing department to handle the documentation needed." He paused for a moment, apparently waiting to see if Kirsten had anything to say. She refused to be drawn, watching his large right hand idly tap a pencil on the polished desk as he appeared to study her. Well, what did he expect her to do? Create a scene?

"Silco can only afford departments that clearly contribute to the total profit picture. . . ."

"The bottom line," Kirsten suggested dryly, throwing out the managerial buzzword with a touch of the contempt she felt for it.

One heavy brow lifted curiously. She guessed he was trying to decide whether or not she was being impertinent.

"As you say, a department must be judged on how much it contributes to the bottom line," he agreed equally dryly, the deep voice reflecting a very soft warning. "And I find little in the way of facts and figures on how the li-

11

brary is doing that," he concluded. He leaned back in the heavy swivel chair and regarded her closely. Without taking his cool hazel gaze off her face, he casually placed his left arm on the desk. The metal hook extending below the white cuff shone gently in the harsh office lighting.

Kirsten's gray-eyed glance flickered in brief, amused curiosity. Was the action his next in the series of intimidating moves he seemed to be making with such calculation? If so, it was a failure. She wondered again how he had lost his hand, knew she would never ask, and proceeded to ignore it. There were more important matters on hand at the moment, such as whether or not her job was worth defending. From a personal angle, it probably wasn't, but there was no denying he had touched her professional pride. Why was it that librarianship, a profession that had a history several thousand years old and that had been instrumental in preserving the history of the human race, still needed defending?

"The reason you haven't come across much information on the library is because your predecessor virtually ignored it, Mr. Kendrick," she stated firmly, and leaned forward to place a thin folder on his desk. The top was so wide, she could not reach far enough to set it directly in front of him, but he obligingly extended his right hand and picked it up.

"I've only been here two months, so there is a lot of hard evidence missing, as you will see. But I've tried to pull together an estimate of engineering time that has been saved because of research done by the library. There is also a section in that report detailing exactly what type of work I perform for the staff. When you read it I think you will find that none of it overlaps the type of work done by the filing section, although I often find it necessary to use their files. The two departments are quite distinct and handle two separate functions. You may, of course, decide that the library's function is not needed, but don't make the mistake of thinking it is redundant." Kirsten didn't bother to phrase her meaning in milder tones, because she was already mentally packing her bags and leaving town. The report she had put in Simon Kendrick's hand was ac-

12

curate, but she thought she already knew enough about the man to guess there was little chance he would understand the value of a company library. Everything she had heard from the gossip mill and had seen for herself fairly shouted that he was hard-bitten corporate management: accustomed to giving orders, determined that profit was the only value, and convinced that his way was the right way. Kirsten didn't care for the type in the least. Privately she decided his arrival was as good a reason as any to check into the job situation on the coast. Seattle was a lovely town, she thought. At least she'd be getting out of this desert!

"Has anyone ever explained the corporate facts of life to you, Miss Mallory?" Kendrick inquired icily as he flipped open the folder and began scanning the thin report inside. Kirsten couldn't help being aware of just how small the document was compared to the rather massive ones stacked on his desk.

"I'm well aware of how everything must be measured in terms of profits, Mr. Kendrick," she replied calmly, gray eyes meeting the steel of his hazel gaze without flinching as he looked up suddenly.

"I'm referring to the managerial hierarchy, Miss Mallory," he returned equally calmly. He glanced down briefly at something she had written in the report and then resumed his intense form of eye contact. "It happens to have its roots in the military structure. . . ." he began, as if about to deliver a lecture.

"That's very unfortunate," Kirsten interrupted feelingly. He couldn't have chosen a less appealing subject, she thought grimly. After Jim Talbot's death Kirsten knew she planned to steer as far from the military world as possible.

"But true, nevertheless," her new manager said firmly, closing the folder gently. "And one of the basic tenets is that lower-ranking members refrain from being impertinent to higher-ranking members!"

Kirsten felt some of the red returning to her face and fought it down with all the mental self-control she could muster. "I've always believed in giving one's loyalty and

13

. . ." She paused to find the right word. "And respect to those who clearly deserve it."

"Then you probably won't go far in the business world," Kendrick shot back smoothly.

Kirsten shrugged, thoroughly irritated now, but she refrained from any more clever remarks. There was always the unfortunate likelihood that she would soon be needing Silco Electronics for a reference.

Having successfully shut her up, Simon Kendrick allowed himself a small smile of victory. "I appreciate the report and will study it thoroughly. Quite frankly I didn't expect you to have something like this pulled together for me."

Kirsten acknowledged the dim compliment with a brief motion of her neat head and waited to be dismissed. Whatever he had originally planned to say when he had requested her presence in his office had apparently been tabled until he read the report. Reluctantly she gave him credit for the effort he seemed to be making toward arriving at a careful decision. It was more than she had expected.

But instead of a nod of casual dismissal, the large man shifted slightly in his chair, the hook out of sight behind the desk, and regarded her openly.

"I understand you came to Richland a short time ago, yourself. Have you been successful in finding an apartment?"

Kirsten stared at him, suddenly quite suspicious. Since when did higher-ranking members of the corporate hierarchy condescend to small talk with lower-ranking members? She knew the answer. When they wanted something.

"I've found a pleasant enough place," she told him cautiously, naming the apartment complex in which she was living and instantly regretting having been careless with the information.

"I've had very little time to hunt for an apartment. It seems as if I've been swamped since the first hour I arrived!" he told her with more feeling than Kirsten would have expected. If the effort at chatting was being made to lower her barriers a little, she decided, it wasn't going to

14

be successful. She'd had too much experience with large, domineering men who thought in military terms.

"Silco has probably put you in the River Inn?" she suggested politely, knowing that's where virtually all of the new high-level employees stayed until they found private residences.

Simon Kendrick nodded, the lines of his mouth turning down expressively as he did so. "I'm growing heartily sick of hotel food already and I've only been there a week. I thought I'd do some serious apartment hunting this weekend. I've been collecting as much information from others as I can so that I don't waste my time looking at unlikely places."

Realizing abruptly that her own complex might now be included on his list, Kirsten decided to remove it from consideration immediately. Some basic female instinct prompted her words, although she hadn't yet acknowledged any genuine danger.

"You would probably want one of the new town-house apartments on the golf course," she suggested quickly, too quickly.

"Oh, I don't need a great deal of space." He smiled pointedly. "And I don't enjoy golf." It didn't occur to Kirsten for an instant that his lack of interest in the sport was in any way due to his missing hand. If Simon Kendrick wanted to swing a club at a small white ball, he would find a way. Probably a very efficient way. "How big are the apartments where you're living?"

"One and two bedrooms," she answered in a small voice, thinking fast. "But the rooms really are small. And the place could use more landscaping. The pool is tiny. During the summer I imagine there won't be room to move in it," she finished on a happier note. Simon Kendrick looked like a man who liked his exercise. He wouldn't be content with doing laps in a postage-stamp-size pool!

"It's almost spring already and I can't even imagine using a pool right now. For a desert, this area certainly isn't very warm," he remarked calmly, never shifting his gaze away from Kirsten's.

15

"But this *is* a desert, you know," she went on as chattily as possible, fighting down a strange trapped feeling. "I've been told the temperature can reach a hundred and ten in July and August." What was she so worried about? From the look of things she probably wasn't going to be around herself this summer! What did she care where this man chose to live? There wasn't any rational reason for it, but Kirsten knew she didn't want Simon Kendrick living near her.

"Good. I've always preferred heat to cold," he told her without batting an eye. Reaching out suddenly with the hook on his left arm, he snagged a memo calendar, drew it close, and jotted down the name of Kirsten's apartment complex. Then he nodded in the dismissal she had been expecting.

"Thank you, Miss Mallory, you've been most helpful. I'll get back to you as soon as I've had a chance to study your report, if not before . . ." He let the sentence end with an unfinished note, almost a speculative note, but Kirsten wasn't paying much attention. She was removing herself quickly and thankfully from his office.

With an automatic smile for Susan Phillips, the efficient older woman Kendrick had selected the first day as his secretary, Kirsten hurried into the corridor and down the stairs of the two-story building to her library. Ben Williamson stuck his elegantly shaggy blond head out of his office and stopped her en route.

"How did it go, Kirsten? Did the ogre take a bite out of you?" Ben's laughing brown eyes met hers and she forced herself to relax. After all, nothing terrible had occurred yet. Why was she so tense?

Casually Kirsten shrugged and smiled back. "Nothing as drastic as a bite, but I wouldn't want to be hanging around at feeding time! I don't think there's a lot of mercy in the man!"

"That goes without saying." Ben grinned. "Why do you think Silco hired him in the first place? You don't send a lamb to do a wolf's job!" His masculine appreciation of an older, tougher man was obvious. In five years, when Ben reached thirty-five, thought Kirsten sarcastically, he proba-

16

bly hoped people would talk about him in the same terms! Men!

"You're right," she finally sighed. "You have to remember I'm more accustomed to the sedate atmosphere of academic libraries where people aren't so inclined to measure accomplishment in money terms. Or if they are, they manage to be more civilized about it!"

"I know, love. Look, it's Friday. Don't forget I'm picking you up around seven for dinner, right?"

Kirsten took in the ingratiatingly friendly smile and nodded agreeably. "I won't forget." For some reason the way Ben's hair curled slightly around his ears reminded her of how severe Simon Kendrick's hair was cut. In both cases, she decided, the haircuts were indicative of the personalities of the two men. Ben was a man a woman would never need to fear, no matter how he hoped to become more like Kendrick! With that thought Kirsten relaxed a little more. She hadn't realized just how tense she had been in the interview.

"See you at seven," she called and continued the rest of the way down the hall. Walking into the one-room library, she discovered an engineer examining a technical manual on transistors and immediately the professional side of her nature took over. Putting Simon Kendrick completely out of her mind, she went forward to help. So many engineers had seemingly never learned to read!

That evening Kirsten took her time getting ready for the date with Ben. He was a good man, she told herself firmly, pulling on sheer panty hose. A man totally different from Jim Talbot, and wasn't that what she wanted? Never again would she get involved with the tough domineering type, she promised herself. That sort of man was all very well in romantic novels, but she had learned the hard way how painful marriage to the type could be. Literally. It would be a long time, if ever, before she forgot the fear and pain of the last night she had seen her husband alive. That had been over three months ago. Jim had been killed in a car accident within a week after she had fled the house in the dark hours of the early morning. She had left

17

with nothing but her clothes and the keys to the car that had been hers before the short-lived marriage.

Taking a deep breath, she put the whole sordid picture out of her head and concentrated on preparing for the evening with Ben. Safe, dependable Ben. Deliberately she selected a long, soft yellow dress that would be pleasant for dancing. Ben was fond of dancing and that suited Kirsten. They had started dating a month ago, although Kirsten knew that was far too soon for a newly widowed bride to be out gallavanting around. But this bride had felt no grief after her husband's death. Only a sense of relief. Besides, few people knew how recent the tragedy had been. She made no secret of her status as a widow, but had carefully allowed people to think more time had passed since Jim's death than was the case. If some wondered why she had gone back to using her own last name, none questioned it to her face. And what business was it of anyone else's?

Kirsten took a last turn before the mirror in the bathroom with its yellow towels hanging from the racks, the yellow shower curtain, and the yellow rug. It was difficult to tell where the bathroom furnishings stopped and the yellow gown began, she thought with a sudden giggle. An objective survey of her slender form revealed nothing new. After twenty-eight years Kirsten had no illusions about the limitations of her own looks. The large, intelligent gray eyes were the best feature of an otherwise pleasant but certainly not beautiful face. The soft brown hair was loose tonight because she knew Ben liked it that way. While certain women had made it clear that at her age she should consider getting a cut, men never complained. As there was nothing particularly outstanding about the rest of her, Kirsten decided, she was entitled to the luxury of wearing her hair any way she liked. It was kept pinned up at work, of course, because it gave her what she considered a more professional look that way. With a small grimace she whirled away from the mirror to answer the sudden knocking on the door.

Ben's happy face when she opened the door was reward enough for the effort she had taken. Apparently she had managed to make herself fairly presentable tonight, Kirsten decided.

"You're looking very tasty, love," Ben told her cheerfully, guiding Kirsten into his small sports car and waiting to close the door until she had gathered in the yellow skirt. Kirsten knew he was going to say that. He always said it.

"And you, as usual, are looking too well turned-out for Richland," she grinned back through the open window. It was true that Ben generally looked modishly dressed. Kirsten suspected that a fair-sized chunk of his salary as an engineer went into his wardrobe and the flashy TR7 in which they now sat.

"I know. I'm wasted on this burg. We both are. What do you say we skip the scintillating evening awaiting us at the River Inn and catch the night flight over to Seattle?" He slid into the seat beside her.

"You're serious, aren't you?" Kirsten laughed, glancing sideways at his handsome, if somewhat soft, profile. He flicked a quick look back at her while shifting out of the parking lot and she thought she detected a note of speculation in the playful brown gaze. Better squelch that in a hurry, Kirsten told herself. Ben was easy to squelch. "Well, I'm sorry, I can't make it tonight. I forgot my flippers!"

"It doesn't always rain in Seattle, Kirsten. And even when it does, people ignore it! Part of the mystique of the city, I'm told!" Ben returned his attention to his driving as he pulled out into the light evening traffic. "Why don't we check it out sometime and get a firsthand report?"

Kirsten hesitated. The invitation was undoubtedly for more than a casual visit to check the weather in Seattle. She had been expecting it and had toyed with different approaches to handling it. But all her answers so far had boiled down to "no." She felt no respect for her late husband's memory, but Kirsten had been too badly hurt, suffered too many doubts about her own judgment, to jump immediately into another serious romance.

"Ben," she began as gently as possible, only to have him toss her a cheeky grin and take the problem out of her hands.

"Don't worry, love. I won't rush you. Can't blame a guy for trying, can you?"

"You know how much I've enjoyed the past month," she smiled back, grateful again for his lighthearted approach to life.

"And that's good enough for now," he finished. "Come on, love, let's show this town what class is all about!" With that he swung the tiny wedge-shaped car into the parking lot of the sprawling hotel overlooking the Columbia River. It was too dark now to see the wide stretch of water that flowed serenely in front of the hotel, but Ben nevertheless asked the hostess for a window table. He always requested a window table. A very predictable man.

The attractive dining room with its floor to ceiling windows and soft lighting hummed in a pleasantly busy fashion. Linen and silver gleamed softly as the staff moved efficiently in response to the usual weekend crowd.

"I feel as if I've memorized the menu," Ben grumbled good-naturedly as he accepted it from the waiter. "It would be worth that trip to Seattle just to eat someplace new!"

"The town's growing. I see they're putting in a new fast hamburger place just down the road! How can you imply a lack of restaurants? That makes five new fast-food places in the past year, I'm told."

"Terrific. And are they going to feature an extensive new wine list?" Ben took the one which was being proffered by the waiter and automatically handed it to Kirsten. "This is the part I look forward to," he confided. "Although as far as my taste buds go, you might as well order jug wine! Will you do the honors again?"

"You may have memorized the menu, but I think I could recite this list in my sleep." She smiled, bending her head to examine the few French offerings. They had already tried the interesting California labels. Ben's willingness to leave the wine selection to her pleased Kirsten. It was one of those things she genuinely liked about him. He wasn't so hung up on the macho routine that he had to try and fake his way through a subject he knew nothing about. When he had discovered she had a real interest in wines on their first date, he had handed her the list and told her to choose. Now he waited patiently while she scanned the list, inquired as to his menu selection, and finally made her choice. By unspoken mutual agreement she always let him handle the routine of accepting the wine from the waiter and tasting it. Instinct told her he would balk at relinquishing the masculine role entirely.

Kirsten set the wine list down and told Ben her decision, helping him with the French pronunciation so he wouldn't embarrass himself, and then something made her glance over her shoulder toward the booths on the other side of the room. A small, shuddery feeling went through her as she caught Simon Kendrick's steady hazel gaze. As usual, he wasn't smiling. He didn't withdraw his attention after he realized she had seen him, but continued to watch Kirsten until she felt herself coloring again. This was the second time he had managed to make her blush, she thought angrily. His manners left a great deal to be desired!

Deliberately she turned back to Ben, finding with a slight start that it was strangely difficult to unlock her gaze from Kendrick's. She watched her escort give the order to the waiter and when he had finished, flashed him her best smile and launched into the task of making herself entertaining.

She was generally very good at promoting casual conversation, privately attributing what social life she enjoyed to her ability to listen and to the fact that there were very few subjects in which she was not interested. The latter fact was the reason she had become a librarian. It had given her a chance to dabble in a variety of fields, such as the nuclear industry in which Silco was deeply involved. The short time she had worked in Richland, however, was rapidly convincing her that nuclear power might well go down on her very short list of subjects she did not care to discuss. At least, not with those like Ben Williamson who were making careers out of it!

"You should have seen her, Kirsten," Ben was saying with laughter. "She really was nervous! Can you imagine?"

"What's wrong with being nervous about nuclear en-

21

ergy?" Kirsten responded carefully, thinking Ben was showing an unusual amount of interest in the new secretary he was discussing. She wondered whether she was soon to have a rival for his somewhat superficial, if pleasant, attentions. She realized the thought was not particularly alarming.

"Blasphemous words in this town, young woman!" he informed her roundly. "Richland was built on nuclear energy! You know that! Why, this whole area didn't even rate a pinpoint on the map until the government moved in during the forties and made it part of the atomic bomb project!"

"And all of its paychecks have been dependent on nuclear projects ever since," Kirsten finished for him, not giving Ben her full attention. A part of her was beginning to be intensely aware of the man seated across the room by himself. Was he still watching her? She dared not turn to look. Would he wander into the lounge after dinner? Somehow she didn't relish having him anywhere near her in the dark intimacy of the cocktail lounge where Ben and she would undoubtedly be dancing later.

"I'm well aware of this town's history, but you're not exactly a long-time resident yourself, Ben. You ought to realize that there are people outside this area who don't buy the whole sales job on nuclear power. The new secretary is obviously one of them." Kirsten finished her comments in a brisker tone than she had intended. It was difficult to keep up a smooth conversation when someone kept staring at you! Instantly she wished she had kept her tone lighter. Poor Ben backed off immediately, as he generally did.

"Okay, okay! I'm in no mood to fight tonight. I've got much better things on my mind!" Ben surrendered laughingly and attacked his salad.

Kirsten followed suit, still wondering if Simon Kendrick would follow them into the lounge. It occurred to her he was not the kind of man to back off.

The wine was the only part of the meal that she really paid any attention to and that was because it was a hobby of hers. By the time they had finished and Ben had suggested they remove to the cocktail lounge, she was feeling unexpectedly tense. Her faint smile took an enormous amount of control as they walked past Kendrick's table. Until now Ben hadn't been aware the other man was in the room, but as they moved toward the door there was no way of missing the large figure seated alone in the booth.

The two men exchanged nods and Kirsten found something inane but polite to say. She prayed that Ben and she would be allowed to pass without more notice but knew it was not to be even as Kendrick eyed her with a lazy gleam in his hard eyes.

"If you two are going in to dance, you must have a drink with me," he announced casually. Kirsten wasn't in the least fooled. The invitation was a command and she and Ben both knew it. They stood aside as their would-be host got to his large feet and picked up the tab lying on the table. Normally the waiter would have handled the check, but Simon Kendrick apparently did not intend to chance losing his victims while going through the formality of paying the bill.

The three of them moved toward the cashier as if nothing in the world was wrong. Ben appeared totally unconcerned. In fact, Kirsten privately thought, he was enjoying being singled out by higher management. But a strange flight of fancy left her feeling rather like a reluctant slave being drawn by invisible chains. Chains that were caught and held casually in the steel grip of a pirate.

CHAPTER TWO

If Ben was aware of Kirsten's uncharacteristic silence as they entered the darkened lounge, he didn't comment on it. She was doing her best to find a few bright, casual remarks, but all she could think about was the tall man who followed politely at her heels.

"How about this table?" Ben suggested, pulling out a chair for Kirsten. "It's far enough from the music that we won't have to shout at each other," he added, indicating the small group tuning their instruments on the slightly elevated stage.

"This is fine," Kirsten announced, sinking thankfully into the seat he held.

With an agreeable nod, Simon Kendrick took the chair to her left, leaving the third for Ben. The table was so small, Kirsten knew it was going to be difficult not to bump each other's arms and knees occasionally. Determinedly she withdrew as far as possible into her chair. It was annoying to have one's evening taken over like this, she thought disgustedly.

"What will you have, Miss Mallory?" Kendrick asked politely. But it was only his words that were polite, she told herself. The way the intelligent hazel gaze pinned her was not. In fact, it made her so self-conscious that she couldn't think clearly enough to recall the names of any of the milder liqueurs she had tried previously. Wine was

24

the only area in which she had any real knowledge of alcoholic beverages.

"Would you like me to choose something for you?" the big man was suggesting smoothly as the cocktail waitress headed in the direction of their table.

"No, that's all right," Kirsten responded hurriedly as she caught sight of a snifter being carried to a nearby table. "I'll have a brandy." She ignored Ben's look of surprise. She hated brandy. But she hated large men presuming to make her decisions for her even more.

One heavy eyebrow lifted in a gesture Kirsten was already finding familiar and then Kendrick turned politely to Ben, noted his request, and gave the order to the rather scantily clad waitress. Kirsten noticed with resentment that she didn't seem the least bit disconcerted by Simon Kendrick. But, then, the silver hook still reposed out of sight on his knee.

The conversation drifted easily into shop talk as they awaited their drinks. Kirsten let Ben carry the burden of the conversation, which he did very handily. A nice man, she told herself for the hundredth time, watching the pleasant-faced young man across from her.

The musicians finished setting up and launched into a fast number that drew several couples from the surrounding tables onto the floor.

"Shall we dance, Kirsten?"

She glanced up to see her date leaning over her and eagerly got to her feet.

"Excuse us." Kirsten smiled at Kendrick, feeling a little guilty about viewing Ben's invitation as an escape but not so guilty as to miss it. He nodded slowly, hazel eyes never leaving Kirsten as she and Ben made their way toward the small dance floor. She knew they didn't because she could feel them.

Once there, Kirsten threw herself into the music, using it to work out some of the tension that had been building within her since she had first noticed Simon Kendrick at dinner. Ben was a willing partner and together they made a lively couple. Both were laughing and breathless when the music eventually drew to a close.

"He's still there," Kirsten hissed at Ben as they moved back to the table.

"I knew he wouldn't give up without a fight," he responded with worldly wisdom.

"What do you mean, give up?" Kirsten demanded, startled. "All he did was invite us for a drink!"

"Correction. He invited you for a drink. And since I was unavoidably attached to you, he had to include me!"

"Ben, don't be an idiot!" Kirsten snapped. "He's all by himself, new in town and feeling a bit lonely. That's all there is to it. It's just our bad luck he picked on us to give him some company." She didn't believe a word of what she was saying.

"That man isn't lonely unless he wants to be," Ben informed her with a grin. "Haven't you seen the looks Liz Wilford has been giving him?"

Kirsten giggled. "I didn't know you paid such close attention to the undercurrents of office romances!"

Ben laughed good naturedly. "You ought to realize by now that in this town office romances are one of the chief forms of entertainment!"

It was on a relaxed, smiling note that Kirsten and Ben reached their host's table and seated themselves. Kendrick had risen politely at their approach and somehow when he sat down again, his chair was even closer to Kirsten's. She felt a strong thigh brush hers as they settled back and she hastily rearranged her legs. Unable to think of anything else in the way of brilliant social moves, she reached for her glass and swallowed a mouthful of the potent, fiery brandy.

The result was predictable and she felt like a gauche teenager taking her first drink of hard liquor when she choked painfully. A sudden blow between the shoulder blades broke the coughing immediately, although it had the secondary effect of nearly sending her sprawling across the tabletop. A vision of herself flying through the air, propelled by Simon Kendrick's casual, lionlike blow, caused her sense of humor to finally return to the fore.

"Kirsten, are you all right?" Ben asked in alarm. A nice man.

26

She shook her head helplessly, trying to keep back the laughter and finally surrendering to it. Ben watched a little anxiously as she succumbed while the man who had caused the entire incident eyed her narrowly. It seemed to Kirsten's light-headed senses that a small smile curled the corners of that firm mouth. Not at all nice.

"Everything back to normal, Miss Mallory?" Kendrick inquired lazily as she got herself under control.

"I'm fine, Mr. Kendrick." Kirsten managed to grin, still gasping a little for air. "Please do me a favor next time you administer first aid, however, and try not to do any permanent damage! I was lucky this time but another rescue attempt might finish me!" She met his eyes and an instant later the humor went out of the situation for her. He had struck her with a fair degree of force. And she realized he'd had no intention of hurting her. But large men often didn't know their own strength. . . . She put the other memory out of her mind and left her smile where it was. But it felt stiff now.

"Next time we'll try another type of brandy, perhaps?" Kendrick suggested outrageously.

"In case you haven't noticed, I'm not all that fond of brandy!" Kirsten retorted promptly. Seizing the opportunity of breaking the disturbing eye contact, she turned on Ben. "Why didn't you say something?" she demanded laughingly. "You know I never drink the stuff. It belongs on pirate ships and in smoke-filled rooms!"

"I always figure you know what you're doing, Kirsten." Ben smiled apologetically.

"A mistaken assumption, perhaps," Kendrick remarked softly.

Kirsten spun around in the swivel chair, all vestiges of humor gone instantly. "Ben's assumption is the right one," she snapped with what she knew was unwarranted ill grace. "I prefer to make my own decisions!"

"Even wrong ones?" Kendrick flicked hazel eyes over her frowning features as if cataloging them for future reference. Her barely concealed displeasure didn't appear to bother him in the least.

"Any kind of decisions," she stated clearly and then signaled Ben that she wanted to dance.

Before her date could respond, however, Simon Kendrick was on his feet. For such a huge person he could move remarkably fast, Kirsten thought ruefully, knowing what was coming and unable to think of a polite way to avoid it.

"I think I deserve some thanks for my gallant rescue," he quipped, giving Ben the benefit of a glance that would have quelled an entire board of directors. "If you have no objections, Williamson?"

There wasn't anything Ben could do and all three of them knew it. Besides, Kirsten sighed inwardly, rising, Ben wasn't exactly the possessive type in the first place. Wasn't that one of the things that attracted her to him? It was simply unfortunate that the very quality she admired in him was the one that would prevent Ben from protecting her against pirates.

Without a word, Kirsten walked ahead of Simon Kendrick toward the dance floor, where the various couples were moving to a slow, languid beat. She wondered briefly how he would solve the problem of holding her with only one hand, thinking of the hook that curled like a sophisticated claw at the end of the left cuff. But she should have known a man like Kendrick would have developed an answer for such a problem. He deftly put both arms around her in an intimate dancing embrace, caging her against his massive, strong body with a suddenness that made her gasp. Instinctively Kirsten resisted, trying to free herself from the enveloping hold, but his only response was to tighten his grasp, making her totally aware of the sheer, powerful masculinity of him in a way that sent a shiver of panic through her. She lifted furious eyes to his and opened her lips to protest.

"It's easier for me this way," he said before she could speak, politely daring her to object.

"Your method of dancing is not particularly comfortable for your partner," she snapped angrily, both hands pushing against his shoulders. "I can barely move my feet!"

"Relax, Miss Mallory," he instructed dryly. "And don't worry about your lack of grace. These shoes can always be reshined and the leather is quite sturdy enough to protect my toes!"

Kirsten fumed inwardly, focusing her smoldering gaze on the sedate pattern of his tie. With an act of will she damped down the flicker of fear.

"Are you laughing at me, by any chance, Mr. Kendrick?" she inquired a little archly, and out of the corner of her eye saw the hard mouth above her curve. She risked a quick glance upward. She couldn't be certain, but in the dim light she had the impression that this time the smile was reaching the hazel eyes.

"I find you delightful, Miss Mallory," he said smoothly, steering her easily around a couple so lost in each other's arms as to be a menace to traffic on the floor.

"Perhaps you're not accustomed to dancing with librarians and are finding the experience a novelty," she remarked with mock sweetness, abandoning the notion of trying to free herself. He seemed totally unaware of her efforts to put more distance between them and she ground her teeth and prepared to suffer through the dance. It couldn't last forever, and safe, undemanding Ben was the one with whom she would be going home.

"It's obvious I have been missing something," Simon agreed feelingly. "May I call you Kirsten?"

She nodded, not knowing what else to do. The request was only a formality anyway. Everyone at Silco and, indeed, in the whole town, was on a first name basis. She had the definite feeling he wouldn't have honored a refusal. She felt his hand move slightly beneath the long hair cascading softly down her back and shivered involuntarily.

"Cold?" he asked with what she knew to be false politeness. Did the man enjoy making a woman nervous? she wondered.

"Hardly. I can barely breathe, however," she told him.

"You'll survive. You look like a nice, healthy young woman," he remarked idly. She knew the hazel eyes were drilling into the crown of her head but Kirsten refused to meet them again. "Getting back to the name business, please call me Simon. Come to think of it, someone told me you're a widow. Should I have been calling you Mrs. Mallory?"

"No!" Kirsten said harshly before she could control her tone. How dare he be so rude!

"Mallory is your former name?" he persisted, not in the least put off, apparently, by her obvious reluctance to continue the conversation.

"That's correct," she replied stiffly. "My husband and I were only married a couple of months, Mr. Kendrick..."

"Simon."

"Simon. Not long enough for me to become used to another name. None of my identification had been changed at the time he died so it was a simple matter to revert to my own name. There's no law against it, you know!"

"Of course there isn't. I merely wanted to get the facts straight. Now try and relax. You can go back to staring at my tie if that will help. The music is almost finished."

"You're too kind, Simon," Kirsten responded tartly. "Your tie is exactly the right level for me!" She lowered her eyes to the vague design again, prompted this time by sheer rudeness.

"About the same level as Williamson's head?" he suggested interestedly.

"Not every woman likes to be overwhelmed and manhandled by someone much larger than she is," Kirsten parried bitingly, refusing to move her gaze upward. She wondered briefly how he had guessed so exactly that she found Ben Williamson a much more comfortable height!

"Some may not like it, but some certainly need it," he shot back easily and then was forced to stop moving as Kirsten came to a complete halt in his arms.

"The dance is over, Mr. Kendrick," she told him firmly.

"Simon," he corrected once more as he released her with obvious reluctance. She felt a momentary tug on a strand of hair as the silver hook seemed to catch in it and then she was free.

Ben's gaze was curiously watchful as Kirsten took her chair. "Enjoy yourselves?" he inquired politely, shifting his glance toward Simon as the man lowered himself care-

30

fully. A man that size undoubtedly had to be extremely cautious around flimsy chairs, Kirsten told herself spitefully. And then felt guilty as the wicked thought caused the return of her smile.

"Very much," Simon answered for both of them, plainly feeling free to speak for Kirsten as well as himself. "I find that that sharp little tongue of Kirsten's keeps a man on his toes, don't you, Ben?" Neither man looked around at their subject's infuriated gasp. They were too busy trading man-to-man glances. Which only served to annoy her further.

"Kirsten has a mind of her own," Ben acknowledged with apparent ease. "It's one of the things I like about her. You can *talk* to her!"

"Thank you, Ben," Kirsten interjected with forced pleasantness. "Remind me to use you instead of Mr. Kendrick for a reference when I start job hunting again!" In an instant she had the undivided attention of both men.

"Job hunting? Do you mean that, Kirsten? You've only been with Silco a couple of months!" Ben was obviously taken aback.

"I think I'm being viewed as a chunk of fat that needs trimming." She smiled innocently, shifting her equally innocent gaze toward Simon. Let him make of it what he wished! The man simply returned her look with a level one of his own that said more clearly than words that she had no business discussing the matter of the library's future at a cocktail table. Kirsten was surprised to find herself wishing she had kept her mouth shut, but refused to let him see it.

"Fat," stated Ben with gratifying firmness, "is one adjective that could never be applied to you!"

"No, but loose-tongued is!" Simon Kendrick said grimly, lifting his glass. For the first time Kirsten saw that he was drinking brandy also. Unwillingly she remembered her own comment that the stuff belonged on pirate ships. Or was it rum that pirates drank? With every ounce of willpower she could summon, Kirsten refused to let her look wander to the softly gleaming steel that served Kendrick for a left hand.

31

"Tell me something, Williamson," the pirate continued with a twist of his hard mouth, "how do you intend to handle this scratchy little kitten?"

"With kid gloves!" Ben chuckled, warm brown eyes meeting Kirsten's, who now felt exactly like the cat Simon Kendrick had labeled her and was finding Ben's glance rather like an affectionate, admiring pat.

"I agree gloves would be useful," her tormentor went on mercilessly, "but I'd suggest velvet ones. With enough iron inside to ensure she doesn't get carried away with nipping the hand that strokes her."

This was too much! Furiously Kirsten whirled on him, nearly upsetting the brandy glass in front of her. "How dare you! Just because Silco thinks you're indispensable and has made the mistake of giving you more power than you ought to have, don't get the idea all of the employees will put up with your sarcasm!" she spat, sounding, she hoped, like an angry woman and not like a snarling cat.

Something very brilliant gleamed in the hazel eyes and she knew she was about to be devastated by a scathing comment. And then salvation appeared in the form of a sleekly dressed, flame-haired woman on the arm of a darkly good-looking man.

"Good evening, everyone!" Liz Wilford's greeting was delivered in the husky, attention-getting voice she had perfected on countless Silco clients. Normally, Kirsten couldn't stand it, but tonight found herself quite happy to hear the seductive tones. "I'd say, fancy meeting you all here, but since there aren't that many places to go in town, I can't really claim to be amazed to find familiar faces, can I? You've all met Roger Townsend? He's one of the managers in the instrumentation department, Simon." Long, beautifully polished nails settled on the arm of Townsend's expensively casual coat.

"We've met," Simon remarked, rising to shake the other man's hand. As usual, he dwarfed the newcomer, just as he dwarfed everyone he came in contact with, Kirsten noticed. But what Roger Townsend lacked in height, he more than compensated for in polished, executive manners and looks. Perfectly styled black hair, sophisticated aviator

32

glasses, and handsome features were accented by a self-confident manner that said clearly that he was a man on the way to the top. Kirsten knew he was well aware of Simon Kendrick's position and had decided that status gave him the right to be treated as an equal. Townsend was very astute when it came to sizing up others. It was one of the talents that was going to assure him future success at Silco. Kirsten was also aware that some people would have characterized his ability as skill in using others, not just sizing them up. She agreed with the assessment and privately thought he and Liz made a terrific couple.

" 'Evening, Simon. I see you've managed to make yourself at home here in the hotel. I sometimes think Silco supports this place!" Roger said genially. "Nice to see you, Kirsten, Ben." He nodded with the proper degree of condescension toward the other two. Kirsten realized that, as irritating as Simon could be, he never conveyed the sense of "position" that Roger Townsend did so well. The touch of pomposity in Liz's escort made Kirsten forget her hostility toward Simon instantly. She found herself wanting to giggle instead. Fortunately, she managed to restrain herself, but not before Simon had noticed. This time when his eye caught hers she was quite certain he was smiling in those hazel depths. For an instant she stared, fascinated, and then Ben's casual conversation brought her back to reality.

"Will the two of you join us?" he was saying, his brown gaze momentarily on the low neckline of Liz's clinging green dress. Kirsten couldn't bring herself to be bothered by his attention and realized with a small sigh that Ben probably wasn't going to be the man to make her fall head over heels in love, after all. Well, hadn't she realized that right from the beginning? Still, he was such a nice, safe man . . .

"Thanks, but we're on our way to the booth over there," Roger replied before Liz could agree. Kirsten knew from the way her green eyes reflected the soft light that the other woman was more than willing to accept the invitation. Liz was the one who deserved to be called a cat, Kirsten muttered to herself, watching Roger guide his date away from the table after a polite good-bye.

For a moment there was silence around the small cocktail table as Kirsten and her companions each waited for the other to make some remark about the sophisticated pair who had just left. Then Kirsten allowed the giggle to escape.

"A perfect couple. They'll go far at Silco," she chuckled lightly, catching Ben's answering smile and knowing he was remembering their earlier comments on office romances. Liz and Roger's had been one of the hotter ones recently.

"Both of them know exactly where they're going," Simon put in, lounging back precariously in his chair and favoring his guests with a mocking smile.

Ben grinned at him. "I have a hunch you're next on Liz Wilford's list should Roger prove unable to sustain the pace!" he warned.

"Surely the worthy Mr. Townsend will continue in first place," Simon responded with a touch of genuine humor that startled Kirsten. She didn't see him as the type to gossip with lower-ranking employees. Although he lacked Townsend's pompous condescension, there was no forgetting Kendrick's dominant presence.

"Not if Liz decides you're going to rise farther and faster," she told him.

"But then, how does she know I intend to rise any farther or faster?" Simon murmured half to himself.

Ben, obviously thinking the answer to that was evident, asked Kirsten to dance again and she accepted willingly.

"Do you think he's ever going to leave?" she demanded, stepping comfortably into Ben's arms.

"Nope. He's prepared to share that table with us for the rest of the evening," Ben stated with great certainty.

"But he only invited us for a drink," Kirsten protested, frowning at him.

"Mr. Kendrick will, in the current business jargon, do 'whatever it takes' to get what he wants, love. And take it from a friend, he's got his eye on you!"

"You're wrong! What could he possibly see in me? I'm

34

not his type at all. Besides, I'm not the least bit interested in him!" Kirsten snapped.

"Calm down, love!" Ben smiled boyishly and hugged her close for a second. "I didn't say he was going to run off with you over his shoulder. Yet, at any rate," he amended teasingly, cocking one blond brow.

"Oh, stop it, Ben!" she commanded pettishly. "You're misreading the situation completely. And even if you were right, I wouldn't be interested! Now cut out the teasing and let's try those new steps you were teaching me last weekend. With any luck he'll excuse himself when we get back to the table."

Whatever Simon Kendrick's reason was for attaching himself to their company, Ben was correct in saying they were stuck with the older man for the rest of the evening. By ten o'clock, Kirsten had danced two more times with Simon, trying to keep control of her tongue on each occasion. It was difficult and there were moments when she actually caught it between her teeth in order to avoid making too sharp a retort. Her sarcasm never seemed to succeed in putting the man in his place, she reflected ruefully. On the contrary, he appeared to thrive on it! Feeling like a martyr, she gave her attention to her feet, determined not to embarrass herself any further by stomping on the man's toes! It had been a long time since she had been forced to move so cautiously on the dance floor. Since eighth grade, Kirsten decided.

"You've become a model of restraint," Simon commented during the last dance she intended to bestow on him. "I admire your self-control."

"Thank you," she replied stiffly, curiously aware of the pressure of his arms against her back. "It's been an effort!"

"My pleasure," he said dryly, using his left arm to haul her even closer.

Kirsten became uncomfortably nervous as his lips hovered somewhere in the vicinity of her ear and then she felt his arm move against her back so that it lay underneath the hair which tumbled softly around her waist. The intimacy of the gestures unnerved her completely. And she was twenty-eight years old, for heaven's sake, she mentally chided herself.

"Mr. Kendrick," she began, determined to gain some control over the situation.

"It's Simon. How many times must I tell you?" he asked softly, not moving his mouth any farther away. The deep, disturbing voice was a husky whisper. It was all Kirsten could do not to tremble in response. She must pull herself together!

"Mr. Kendrick," Kirsten insisted, tightening her muscles in preparation for pulling away from his big, hard body. "I barely know you and I have an aversion to dancing like this with someone I've met so recently! Please take me back to the table!" For a long, excruciating moment she didn't think he was going to do as she asked and then she was free and they were threading their way through the maze of tiny, intimate cocktail tables.

Without taking her seat, Kirsten sent a speaking glance toward Ben, who responded with gratifying obedience.

"I guess we'd better be on our way, huh, Kirsten?" he said quickly, rising almost at once. "It's getting late. . . ."

"It's only a little after ten, Williamson," Simon told him silkily and turned toward Kirsten. "Surely you're not going to concede defeat so readily, Miss Mallory?" he added with all the ease of a knife slipping into butter. Or between ribs, she thought with revulsion.

"I wasn't aware we were engaged in a contest, Mr. Kendrick. I'm glad to learn exactly how you view the situation, though. I intend to withdraw at once and leave the field to you. If that gives you a sense of victory, you're welcome to enjoy it." Without waiting to see if Ben was following, she turned on her heel and walked proudly out of the lounge. Hasty excuses and quick steps behind her told Kirsten that Ben was not going to abandon his date, even if she was behaving strangely. A nice guy.

"What's gotten into you, Kirsten? That man is going to have a lot to say about our future with Silco, you know! He may be a bit of a wolf, but you're a big enough girl to handle that!" Ben took her arm as they walked through the hotel lobby. Kirsten paid no attention to the replicas of

36

Northwest Indian carvings that lined the walls, and made straight for the wide glass doors that opened onto the darkened parking lot.

"You were right this afternoon when you said Silco gave us a wolf to do a wolf's job!" she snapped, not looking at Ben. "But I hope you don't intend to sink to Liz Wilford's level and try to make friends with him. He'll still gobble you up if the mood takes him!"

"Ah, come on, Kirsten." Ben settled her wrap over her shoulders as they came to a halt in front of his car. She had completely forgotten it in her hasty departure, not being accustomed to leaving scenes in high dudgeon. Which meant she'd led too sheltered a life, Kirsten reflected.

"Aren't you taking this a little too seriously?" Ben continued, opening the door. "All the man did was dance with you a few times . . ." He broke off as she glared at him. Kirsten was very, very certain she wanted only easy-going, good-natured men like Ben in her life and not the overwhelming, giant-sized ones, but there were times, she told herself, when it would be pleasant if the Ben types were a little more protective! Well, you can't have everything, she reminded herself firmly, and she didn't need a man's protection from another man! She could take care of herself.

"Let's go home, Ben," she said quietly. "It's been a long evening!"

"Kirsten, it's too early! There are other places in town. What do you say we try the lounge at the Washington Room? They've got a new disco band, Jess told me this afternoon. . . ."

One look at the pleading expression in those brown eyes and Kirsten gave in. She didn't have the heart to spoil Ben's evening even if she was more than ready to call it a night.

"All right," she smiled, trying to lighten her mood for his sake. "Let's go."

It was nearly one o'clock in the morning when Ben finally deposited her at the front door of her apartment. He hung around hopefully for a nightcap invitation, but this

time Kirsten was firm. It had been a long week and she was tired. All she craved now was her bed.

"Maybe I'll see you over the weekend?" he suggested half-heartedly as he leaned forward to give Kirsten a peck on the cheek. He had aimed for her mouth but at the last moment she evaded him. As she usually did.

"We'll see, Ben," Kirsten temporized. "I really should catch up on my housework. . . ." Talk about a lame excuse, Kirsten thought mockingly!

"Yeah, well, maybe I'll give the new secretary a call," he commented slyly, as if waiting to see how she'd take the hint of competition. Like a small boy, Kirsten thought with a flash of humor.

"Joyce Osborne? I think that would be very nice. She hasn't had a chance to meet anyone yet," she told him cheerfully. No man, not even a nice one like Ben, was going to think Kirsten Mallory responded to threats like that!

Ben sighed, apparently abandoning the effort. "All you're looking for is a friend, isn't it, Kirsten?" He smiled in a woebegone fashion, but the brown eyes didn't reflect any real hurt and Kirsten's mouth curved gently.

"Yes, Ben. Just a friend."

"I was beginning to realize that." He took a deep breath and stuck out his hand. "Well, I'll say good night, *friend!*" His grin was genuine if a trifle forced.

Kirsten shook it gratefully and then waved good-bye with a sense of relief before opening her apartment door. The soft hum of the aquarium pump was the only sound in the darkened room and the fluorescent light above the tank provided the sole light source. Kirsten groped for a moment and found the hall switch.

For an instant the disaster didn't register. She had told Ben she needed to catch up with her housekeeping but this was ridiculous! Chaos reigned. From where she stood Kirsten could see turned-out drawers, upended chairs, torn cushions, and a broken lamp. She couldn't believe it! Kirsten simply stood there, staring for what seemed an eternity before she was startled out of her trance by the sound of a swift, hard knock on the door behind her.

Coming as it did after her discovery, and seldom having

callers at this hour of the night, Kirsten felt she couldn't be blamed for jumping a good two inches. Her heart thumped into high gear and breathing became difficult. She wished very badly that she kept dogs—large dogs—instead of tropical fish. The knock sounded again and, feeling like an idiot, she asked who it was.

"It's Simon, Kirsten. I want to talk to you."

It was the final straw. The wolf was now at her door and her sanctuary had just been shown to be very insecure!

CHAPTER THREE

Kirsten opened the door a fraction and peered out. In the pale light of a street lamp he stood tall and solid on her doorstep. His right hand was curled into a fist, but the look on his face wasn't hostile.

"What do you want?" she whispered.

"For God's sake don't look at me like that," Simon muttered. "I came by to return this." The right hand uncurled, revealing a small golden circlet.

"My earring! I didn't know I'd lost one . . ." Automatically she raised one hand to her right ear, where she was suddenly conscious of a tiny, missing weight. It was a measure of her dazed condition, Kirsten thought, that she could actually pay attention to the fact that she'd lost an earring. "Thanks for returning it," she added hurriedly, reaching one hand through the narrow crack in the door to retrieve her property.

Instantly Simon's hand withdrew to the safety of a coat pocket.

"Can I come in for a few minutes? I only want to talk to you," he asked softly, hazel eyes pinning her nervous gray ones.

"I . . . I can't talk now! The house is a mess and I . . ." Good lord! Since when had she become the master of the understatement? "I have things to do. . . ." Like call the police!

"Just for a moment, Kirsten, please!"

The wolf begging at her door now? What a night this was evolving into!

"What the hell is wrong? Has something happened?" Simon demanded suddenly, all note of pleading gone instantly from his voice. "Let me in, Kirsten! It's obvious you've got trouble and I can help."

Without further ado, Simon's right hand settled on the door and pushed inward. There was no way Kirsten could fight that strength. Helplessly, she stepped aside and let him into the small, tiled hall.

"What's the matter? Williamson didn't give you any trouble, did he? It looked to me like you got rid of him pretty easily . . ." His words broke off as he caught sight of the shattered room beyond. He swore swiftly and concisely and then he didn't waste any more time swearing. He turned so abruptly that Kirsten instinctively stepped backward, only to be brought up short by the door against her back.

"You just walked in to find this?" he demanded, gesturing vaguely with his right hand toward the living room.

"I realize I'm not the world's best housekeeper, but I do have slightly higher standards than this mess indicates," she managed pertly.

"You haven't had time to call the police yet, have you? No, you couldn't have. I came as soon as Williamson left." He finished his own question. "Have you touched anything, Kirsten?" he demanded, turning once more to survey the chaos. For some reason she noticed that the steel hook was out of sight in his coat pocket and had been since she'd opened the door. Kirsten knew he wasn't overly self-conscious about it normally. He wasn't the type to worry about what others thought. Had he hidden it because he thought it might bother her?

"Did you hear me, Kirsten? Have you touched anything yet?" He still wasn't looking at her and she realized he was now all business regardless of what he might have had on his mind when he knocked on her door.

"No, nothing. I haven't had a chance to do anything," she answered swiftly. "I was about to call the cops when

41

you knocked. I can't even begin to imagine who would do something like this," she went on, drawing strength as she talked. Talking about it made it all seem so much more normal, somehow. "One of my neighbors has had trouble with obscene phone calls, but that's the extent of problems I've heard about in this complex." Slowly she moved away from the door and tried to push past his bulk in the hall. Almost absently he reached out to stop her.

"I'll call," he informed her firmly. "In the meantime, don't touch a thing, understand? I suppose we'd better make sure whoever did this is gone first. Stay right here and don't move. Scream the building down if you so much as see your own shadow. Clear?" Pausing to see if his words had sunk in, he smiled and left to make a quick foray through the small apartment.

He smiled, Kirsten thought ludicrously. Maybe he's used to this sort of thing! She stayed put while he made the rounds and then returned to her side, striding quickly through the clutter.

"Okay, honey, where's the phone?" He glanced at her inquiringly, one reddish-brown brow raised.

"The phone, Mr. Kendrick, is in the bedroom," Kirsten said austerely, reacting immediately to his casually used term of endearment.

"Back to the Mr. Kendrick, are we?" He grinned briefly and then disappeared into the hall leading to the bedroom.

Kirsten picked her way toward the couch and sat down carefully on a torn cushion. She had just barely been able to pay for it, she remembered gloomily, thankful she'd had the foresight to buy some insurance the previous month.

"The cops will be here shortly," Simon announced, coming back into the living room. Then he favored her with a quick grin. "I had a tough time telling the yellow phone apart from the yellow bedclothes around it!"

"I like yellow," Kirsten replied calmly, refusing to defend her color preference. "Did they tear up the bedroom as much as the rest of the place?" she added with concern and marveling at her own outward calm.

"No. The bedclothes were pulled off the bed, hence my difficulty in locating the phone, and the closet shelf was gone through, but that's about it. It looks like time may have been running out at that point. . . ." He seemed to realize suddenly that she was sitting very stiffly on the couch and the hazel eyes narrowed slightly.

"It is all right if I sit here, isn't it? I mean, I wouldn't want to spoil any clues," she asked brightly, having no intention of moving anyway. It was, after all, her apartment, and she needed the support at the moment!

"Kirsten?" he said worriedly. "Are you all right? You're not about to go hysterical on me, are you?"

"Heavens, no!" she assured him feelingly. "Wouldn't think of it. You might decide to use that old remedy of slapping my face or something equally unpleasant! Besides, can't you see I'm taking this all rather well?"

He grinned again. She was amazed at what the look of pleasure did for that harsh face. "You're taking it beautifully, honey. Which doesn't surprise me in the least. I knew the second you walked through my door this afternoon that you had plenty of guts!"

"Please," she winced. "How about calling it spirit? Guts sounds so . . . so . . ." She trailed off, unable to find the right description.

"So crude?" he supplied, stepping over an overturned end table to join her on the couch. "Sorry. Sometimes my language doesn't always reflect the purity of my thoughts!" The abused furniture sagged under his weight.

Kirsten swung her gaze around to assess the sober, serious expression that masked his features and then caught the gleam in the hazel eyes. She couldn't help it; her sense of humor surfaced and she laughed.

"Tell me about the purity of the thoughts you must have had when you knocked on my door this evening!" she ordered.

"I like those gray eyes of yours when you giggle," he observed, ignoring her question.

"It's the contact lenses. They add a certain sparkle," she told him dryly.

"Some other time I'll tell you more about your certain sparkle," he remarked. "At the moment I suppose we ought to be discussing this little incident." He nodded toward Kirsten's welcome-home surprise. "Is there anything I should know before the police arrive?"

"If you're trying to ask me if I have the slightest idea who would do such a thing, forget it. I've only been in town a couple of months and I haven't had time to make many enemies!"

"And no dark secrets following you from your previous life?" he persisted with deceptive lightness.

She looked away from those gleaming eyes and shook her head.

"No secrets," she said firmly. And it was the truth. The one man who had hurt her was dead. She was safe.

"Well, maybe the police will have some ideas," Simon said thoughtfully, leaning back to rest his left arm along the back of the couch. The action made Kirsten nervous. Another short move would have that arm around her and then what would she do?

With an abrupt little jump, she got to her feet and was trying to think of a polite explanation for her behavior when someone knocked at the door.

"That will be the cops," Simon announced, getting casually to his feet and starting toward the door. "I'll get it."

"Don't start making yourself too much at home," Kirsten muttered between clenched teeth, but she couldn't tell if he had heard her.

The police were everything one hopes police will be when one needs them: sympathetic, efficient, professional. But Kirsten could tell when they left an hour later that they were as much at a loss for an explanation as she was. Simon stood beside her in the doorway and watched the patrol car pull out of the parking lot at around two-thirty. Kirsten sighed as the taillights disappeared.

"I have the feeling this is going to remain one of those unexplained acts of vandalism you read about occasionally in the newspapers," she groaned, making no move to go back inside the apartment. Hopefully, Kendrick would take his cue and leave now. He seemed larger than ever standing next to her.

"Maybe," he shrugged. "The cops were probably right. If you really can't come up with the names of any suspi-

44

cious characters, I guess we'll have to let it ride for now."
He moved to go back inside.

Kirsten panicked.

"Well, thanks for the help in dealing with the police,"
she began nervously, remaining where she was in the doorway. "It's getting rather late. I'll take care of this mess in
the morning. . . ."

"Good idea," he agreed. "I'm ready to hit the sack, myself." But he didn't head for his car, he continued on into
the living room and began fluffing the couch cushions.

"Close the door, Kirsten, it's getting cold in here," he
advised, standing back to eye his handiwork.

"I'll close it as soon as you're gone," she told him
pointedly, beginning to shiver from the cold. He was right.
It was freezing outside. She folded her arms protectively
around herself and waited.

"I thought I'd spend the night," he remarked, as if he
did it regularly. "This disaster is bound to make you
uneasy. You'll feel better knowing I'm out here in the living room. This couch is a little short, though, isn't it?"

"No!"

"Well, maybe not for someone your size, but for me it's
going to be small," he responded decidedly, nodding his
dark head thoughtfully. So far he hadn't looked at her,
giving his full attention to the matter of his bedding.

"Simon Kendrick, you are not spending the night here!
I want you to leave—at once! Do you hear me? Simon,
pay attention to me! I'll call the manager and have you
thrown out if you don't do as I say!" Kirsten was furious
and no longer making any effort to be polite. She wanted
this big man out of her apartment and out of her life! It
was getting colder and colder with only the protection of
the light yellow dress, but nothing could have induced her
to step inside and close the door.

Nothing, that is, except a huge man who was capable of
lifting her bodily out of the doorway and well into the
hall. Which is exactly what Simon Kendrick did before
she could blink an eye. It wasn't fair that a man his size
could move so quickly. And it was even more galling that
he managed the whole operation with only one hand. She

felt completely helpless as that right arm closed around her waist, hoisted her unceremoniously into the air, and then set her down as if she were a bag of groceries. By the time she caught her breath the door had been firmly closed and Simon was standing between it and Kirsten, eyes glittering with laughter and something else. Something that really awakened the fear within her. With all the dignity she could muster, Kirsten refused to let it show.

"Relax, honey. I'm not going to hurt you," he soothed.

Kirsten absorbed the rocklike stance he had adopted in front of her and closed her hands into small fists.

"Simon, this is my place," she whispered as coolly as possible. "I want you to leave. You have no right acting like this!" Then the coolness seeped out of her tone to be replaced by a touch of demanding defiance. "Isn't there any trace of the gentleman in you?"

"Why do you bother to ask? You've already decided there isn't, haven't you?" He smiled coldly, the warmth fading from those eyes, but not the intention. The little twist of fear inside Kirsten grew. Simon came forward slowly, forcing her to back into the living room. Beyond him the door was so inviting. . . . She began weighing her chances.

"Don't bother, Kirsten," he told her off-handedly. "I'll catch you before you take three steps."

She surrendered the possibility of that escape route and, turning, stalked farther into the room. With a certain grim calculation, she mentally ticked off the various appeals left to try.

"This is still a small town in many ways, Simon, even if it has been growing so rapidly lately. I know my neighbors and there will be gossip if you stay here. You can count on it reaching Silco, too!" She went to stand in front of the fish tank. Thank God the vandals hadn't used a hammer on it, she thought feelingly. It was calming to watch Jeremiah the Algae Eater going about his business of keeping the tank sides clean.

Simon came to stand behind her, not touching. "We needn't concern ourselves with gossip, honey. Your friends will understand that I couldn't leave you alone after what's happened."

"And how am I supposed to explain the fact that you appeared on my doorstep at one o'clock in the morning when everyone knows I had a date with Ben?" Kirsten hissed angrily, still watching the graceful motions of the fish. "For that matter, what the hell were you doing there—here—at that hour?" She hugged her arms around herself again and flinched as his hand touched her hair lightly, almost appealingly. Automatically, Kirsten corrected herself. Simon Kendrick would never plead for anything. Much less a woman's attention. The impressions she'd had briefly when she'd opened the door earlier and again just now when he stroked her hair were false ones. He probably cultivated that particular approach to put unsuspecting women off their guard!

"I told you, I came to return your earring," Simon said softly, fingers entwining themselves more deeply in her hair.

"I don't believe you. It could have been returned on Monday at work."

"I also wanted to talk to you. . . ."

"You could have called in the morning. Simon, stop lying to me! Do you think I'm a fool? What is it about me that makes men think they can treat me . . ." Kirsten broke off and whirled to face her tormentor, jerking her hair loose from his fingers. "Why are you here, Simon Kendrick?" She wished mightily she didn't have to look up so far in order to meet his eyes.

"I'm here for all the reasons I told you, Kirsten," he began, eyes stern and a fine degree of roughness in the deep tones of his voice. "I'd never, ever lie to you. But I do admit there was another reason."

"I can't believe you're so desperate for a woman that you would set out to annoy an employee!" she blazed, trying desperately to forestall any protestations of desire from him.

"I'm not desperate for just any woman," he growled, wrapping his huge hand around the back of her neck and holding her absolutely immobile while his eyes bored into

47

hers. "I want you," he added very distinctly. "And the main reason I was waiting when you got home tonight was to see if I was going to have to pull that puppy Williamson out of your bed!"

Kirsten gasped, a combination of fury and astonishment driving out the fear momentarily.

"You're out of your mind! You hardly know me, and my relationship with Ben Williamson is none of your business!"

"It became my business today when you walked into my office acting as if you could care less what I did with your job," he grinned, the tiny lines at the corners of his eyes crinkling. "I intended to call you in the morning, but when you appeared at dinner I decided not to let such a heaven-sent opportunity pass!"

"And so you parked yourself outside my door and waited until I got home from a date with another man so that I could fall immediately into your arms?" Kirsten breathed scathingly, trying to dislodge his grip on her neck. "If you aren't careful, you're going to throttle me!"

"Never!" he said with great certainty. "I've told you I'd never hurt you. And I didn't exactly expect you to fall into my arms tonight, either. I planned to talk to you. That's all!" Then he added, deadpan, "Of course, if my talking had convinced you to throw yourself at me, so much the better!"

"You're impossible! Nobody makes up his mind about another person that fast!"

"I do."

"Really? And how often during the past, let's say, year or so, have you made up your mind that you wanted a particular woman?" she mocked, feeling desperate.

"If you're asking if I've lived a celibate life waiting for you, the answer is no," he admitted cheerfully. "But there's a difference between enjoying oneself and really wanting someone!"

Where have I heard that before, Kirsten thought bitterly. "Isn't there just, though? And you know the difference?"

"I discovered it today," he stated with satisfaction, finally removing his restraining hand. Kirsten breathed an unconscious sigh of relief and noted that the hook was still tucked politely out of sight in a jacket pocket. "I think it's time we went to bed, don't you?" he added conversationally. "Where are the extra blankets? Hall closet?" He was already striding toward the hall that led to the bedroom, leaving Kirsten standing, frozen, in front of the aquarium. My God! What was she going to do?

She watched disbelievingly as he helped himself to blankets, filched an extra pillow from her bed, and came back into the living room. He set about making the couch into a bed with suspicious dexterity. A skill he'd learned in the military? Kirsten shuddered. She watched with a sort of mesmerized helplessness as he finished the job and turned back to face her, right hand already at the knot of his tie.

"Going to stay and watch?" Simon inquired humorously, knowing full well he could face her down.

Kirsten seethed with righteous anger, knowing she was in a classic no-win situation. She couldn't possibly remove him herself, and if she called the police to do the job, there was no telling how bad a scene Simon might create. Unless he actually made a serious move to threaten her physically, she didn't think she could bring herself to scream. And she sensed he knew it.

"Someday," she vowed with an intensity of feeling she hadn't known she possessed, "you're going to regret this!" She swung away, toward the bedroom.

"I'll use the bathroom first," he called after her. "Then you can take your time."

Kirsten's response was to slam her bedroom door. Feeling a little safer now, she reached out and locked it. The task reassured her considerably. As long as she stayed here she would be safe, she decided, and eyed the window by the bed as a possible escape route. Immediately she regretted having left the keys to the car in her purse, which was decidedly out of reach unless she wanted to risk another trip to the living room. The car had been her means of escape before and she'd use it again if she had to, but, damn it! She was getting tired of running away from powerful, domineering men! She had her rights! And she was

49

going to have to start sticking up for them! Tensely, she began to pace the carpet beside the bed.

"So," she muttered to herself, "how are you going to get rid of that man out there?" Small rustling sounds came from the bathroom and Kirsten gritted her teeth, wondering if he carried spare toothbrushes in his pocket for these sorts of occasions. How often did he encounter women he "desperately" wanted, anyway? Her temper rose to the boiling point and the necessity for some physical action drove her over to the window.

Peering between the curtains, she studied what could be seen of the parking lot. Her own tiny compact wasn't visible from here but there was an unfamiliar Mercedes in one of the slots. Simon's? A big car for a big man, she reflected bitterly.

A casual knock on her bedroom door drew her startled attention. Was he going to force his way in here? The door didn't look as sturdy as it had a few minutes ago. Well, she'd use the window if he tried anything, Kirsten decided grimly.

"What do you want?" she called, trying to control the trembling of her voice.

"Just wanted to let you know the bathroom's free," he called back easily. "Good night, Kirsten. See you in the morning!" His footsteps retreated in the direction of the living room and Kirsten sank down on the bed with relief, noting absently that he'd done a bit of straightening in this room earlier when he had used the phone. The sheets and blankets were back on the bed, at least. The contents of the closet shelf still lay scattered about on the carpet, though.

It was late and Kirsten realized she was exhausted. This was her bedroom and her apartment. She was not going to let herself be chased away. And if she heard so much as a squeak near her door during the night, she would scream until a neighbor called the management!

But it would have taken considerably more than a squeak to awaken her that night. Kirsten wasn't aware of anything after her tousled head hit the pillow until pale, early spring sunlight filtered through the curtain the next morning. Accompanied by the wonderfully beckoning smell of freshly brewed coffee.

It was the coffee aroma that brought Kirsten out of her dreams and back to reality. Suddenly wide awake, she flung back the covers and padded to the closet, hunting for a robe. She took her time getting ready, trying to work up nerve to face her houseguest. Grateful not to encounter him in the hall, she scurried to the bathroom and back and then slipped into jeans, a long-sleeved shirt, and a casual pair of shoes. Then, unable to decide what to do with her long hair, she settled for the usual weekend style and braided it, securing the ends with rubber bands saved from evening newspapers. Finished, she opened her door and went bravely down the hall toward the unfamiliar sound of someone making himself very much at home in her own kitchen.

In the light of day, the vandalism didn't look quite so bad as it had the previous evening. Then Kirsten realized that was because Simon had been busy. The furniture had been righted, books replaced, the broken lamp removed. She moved through the living room and came to a halt in the doorway of the small, sunny kitchen.

"Good morning, honey. How did you sleep?" Simon demanded cheerfully as he pawed through a drawer with his right hand. "Where do you keep the spatula?" Kirsten noticed he had replaced the two drawers that had been completely removed and emptied the previous evening.

She considered a moment. "Try that one, near the stove." Then she continued on into the little room. "On second thought, forget it. This is my kitchen and I'll do the cooking. Even if the guests are uninvited!"

"I was hoping you'd volunteer," he grinned, not the least abashed. "I've got the coffee going, though. Does that win me a gold star?"

Kirsten gave him a brief appraisal as he lounged his solid bulk against the refrigerator. Except for the shadow of a morning beard, Simon Kendrick appeared to be in disgustingly good shape. Not at all as if he had spent the night on a too-short couch. Perhaps he was accustomed to spending nights in places other than his own bed, she thought sarcastically. He was still wearing the slacks from last evening but the coat had been discarded and one sleeve of the white shirt rolled to the elbow in preparation for kitchen duties. The silver hook extended with a quiet authority from the other sleeve. He didn't seem to be so concerned with keeping it out of sight this morning, Kirsten realized fleetingly, and briefly wondered why. It was as if he had reached the conclusion that it didn't bother her.

"After that stunt last night, I'm not sure anything could get you a gold star. Maybe a medal of honor for managing to find the coffee makings in this mess, but not the gold star!" she announced decisively.

"I'll take a good-morning kiss, instead," he said softly, and before she knew what was happening he detached himself from the refrigerator and, taking one large stride forward, folded her into his huge embrace. Kirsten felt like a butterfly being trapped in a net.

"No!" she managed to get out, and then his mouth was covering hers in a kiss that began as a huge, gentle, questing thing but abruptly exploded into a persuasive, sensuous, passionate demand unlike anything she had ever known. For a long moment Kirsten felt quite stifled with astonishment and then she began to lose herself in Simon's arms. Her lips were irresistibly forced apart until the warmth of his mouth made her moan slightly. With a floundering, drowning feeling she made an effort to push him away, her hands splayed against his massive chest. He seemed totally unaware of her efforts, merely pulling her closer as if he would taste all of her there in the morning sunlight. Kirsten wasn't even conscious of the moment when her arms gave up the struggle and wrapped themselves around his waist.

Her response seemed to trigger a deeper need in him and even as she felt herself molded more closely against the toughness that was Simon, the quality of his kiss deepened yet again in a dizzying, plunging way that was frightening. The fear brought her back to reality.

"Simon, no! Please let me go!" she begged as his lips freed her mouth to attend to her throat.

"Don't ask me to stop, Kirsten," he whispered in a low, husky voice which seemed to come from deep in his chest. "I want you so badly . . ."

"You want me!" she snarled, suddenly pulling her hands back to place them flat against his chest again. "That's supposed to be enough, is it? The fact that you want me? Well, it isn't! Not nearly enough!" Kirsten pushed with all her strength and couldn't budge him. But she had his attention now. Simon lifted his head to gaze down into her angry face and she saw some of the passion fade from the hazel eyes to be replaced by a softer expression.

"Why are you so afraid? I promise I'll make you want me, too, It won't be all one-sided, honey." He ignored her pushing hands as if they weren't there, his tones deliberately soothing, which further irritated Kirsten. "You can relax and enjoy the relationship. I would never hurt you."

"Don't talk to me about 'relationships'! I'm not in the mood for the kind of relationship you have in mind and I never will be! When I fall in love it will be with a kind, gentle, *small* man who can't pick me up with one hand! One who won't try to rush me into a whirlwind 'relationship'! Is that understood?" She met his steady look determinedly, wishing desperately she hadn't just used the word love and willing him to ignore that phrase.

"Let me get all this straight," he said carefully, but not angrily. Nor did he release Kirsten while he ran through his logic. "You aren't interested in a relationship based only on, let's call it 'physical need,' shall we? And you want a man your own size." The hard lines around his mouth relaxed in a tiny smile. Kirsten refused to return it.

"Five foot four is a very respectable height," she gritted.

"It's just right. For you," he agreed readily.

"My neck is getting sore trying to talk to you now," she pointed out. Instantly his right hand moved up to start massaging that portion of her anatomy and Kirsten wished she had kept her mouth shut. She still wasn't free.

"The basic idea," she said very distinctly, "is that I prefer men who don't try and use their superior physical strength to get their way."

"And you want one who's passionately in love with you, don't forget," he added, his hand moving strongly against her neck. The hazel eyes studied every square centimeter of her taut expression.

"Yes!" Was that really so much to ask? she wondered.

"Would you believe me if I said I meet at least one of the conditions? That of being in love?" His words were low, sensuous.

"Of course not! You barely know me!" Kirsten replied sturdily.

"Ummm. So I guess I can forget that approach for a while, right? There's not a whole lot I can do about my size," he continued musingly.

"True." She pounced on that.

"I could promise not to haul you around with one hand. But one hand is all I have," he noted, a gleam entering the stern gaze. A gleam that was instantly replaced with a curious, questioning look. "Does the hand, or rather, lack thereof, bother you, Kirsten?" he asked with such totally unexpected vulnerability that she answered him immediately, honestly, without pausing to think.

"No, of course not! What bothers me is what you do with the one you have!" she grumbled and was rewarded with a pleased smile. Right away Kirsten acknowledged to herself that she had just made a bad mistake. It would have been expedient to have used Simon's one-handedness as an excuse. She felt like an idiot for having been trapped into such a quick answer, but then was forced to admit that she would never have been able to bring herself to use it against him. Lying had always been an exceptionally difficult skill for Kirsten and the clear eyes reflected that.

"Now that's settled," he remarked, leaving her to wonder what, exactly, had been settled. "I have to tell you I'm in a hell of a hurry for you, Kirsten, honey. I'm too old to waste time going through all the crazy, teasing, courting rituals and you're not getting any younger, yourself. . . ."

"Thank you very much!" she snapped, stung.

"It's the truth, isn't it? You're what? Twenty-seven? Twenty-eight? And I'm thirty-seven. Why should we play

54

games? That's for kids like Williamson or for someone like Liz Wilford . . ."

"She's not that much younger than I am!" Kirsten protested, feeling quite put upon now. Her gray eyes narrowed as Simon roared with outright laughter. His laughter was a very huge thing, well fitted to the rest of him.

"You see how poor I am at the business of wooing!" he remarked when he had himself under control again.

"Simon," she began furiously, but was interrupted by a knock on the door.

For an instant Kirsten was paralyzed. Good lord! What was she going to do? How could she ever explain Simon's presence to Ben or anyone else?

Simon took one look at her stunned face and firmly set her aside. Before she could stop him he was at the door. Kirsten nearly collapsed with relief when the mailman handed him a package and disappeared.

"See? Nothing to get flustered about," he announced brightly, covering the distance to the kitchen in a few large steps. Kirsten took the package he thrust at her and numbly began fumbling with the wrapper.

"Even if it had been someone you know, what's the harm? Your friends will have to find out about me sooner or later," he continued with satisfaction, watching Kirsten as she worked on the package.

"There is nothing for anyone to find out," she insisted feelingly and then glanced again at the outside wrapper.

The original address had sent it to the town where she had lived as Mrs. Jim Talbot for such a short period of time. The block letters had been scratched out and a new hand had sent it to her father's address in California. That, too, had been partially obliterated and the last direction was in her father's neat handwriting. He was the only one who knew her current whereabouts, she reflected.

With a sense of foreboding, Kirsten finished tearing off the brown paper and examined the shoebox inside. She was aware of Simon's gaze over her shoulder as she lifted the cover and stared at the contents.

Inside the box were a medal (from Vietnam, she knew), a Zippo lighter, and an envelope with her name on it. "Why in the world would anyone send me Jim's things?" Kirsten said disbelievingly.

CHAPTER FOUR

"These are probably some of what are usually called the 'effects of the deceased,'" Simon remarked, reaching into the box to lift out the medal. "Someone must have found them and decided you should have them." He fingered the decoration curiously. "Purple Heart? Your husband was in Vietnam?"

Kirsten nodded. "Long before I met him. I don't even know what sort of wound he received. Whatever it was, he recovered."

"What service?"

"The Marines," she told him bitterly. "What else?"

"Why do you say it that way?" Simon demanded, a strange glint in his eye that Kirsten recognized instantly.

"Oh, God! Not another one!" she groaned. "I should have guessed. What rank?" she added despairingly.

"Captain," he said, sounding somewhat apologetic. As well he should be, Kirsten told herself.

"It figures. Here, give me that," she said crisply, reaching for the medal. "Let's get something to eat. I'm starving." That was a lie, but she was desperate to change the conversation.

"Aren't you going to read the letter?" Simon was already moving his large hand back into the box before she could move it out of the way.

"Nope. If you want to know what I'm going to do with

these things, I'll show you!" Putting the lid back on the shoebox after snatching the letter from him, she dumped the whole thing into the kitchen garbage.

"Hey, wait a minute! What about his folks? Maybe they'd appreciate having that stuff," Simon protested.

"As far as I know, Jim had no living relatives. What do you want for breakfast?" Kirsten opened a cupboard door and pulled out the skillet. "Omelets okay?" Perhaps food would distract him!

"Fine," he replied absently, his gaze on the garbage bag in the corner. "Maybe you ought to at least read the letter . . ."

"What is this? The old Marine esprit de corps coming to the fore? I will make one final pronouncement on the subject of Jim Talbot and that's it!" Kirsten turned away from the stove to face Simon momentarily, hands on hips. "He was a first-class bastard. Within a week of my marriage to him I knew I'd made the biggest mistake of my life. My only regret is that it took me almost two full months to work up the courage to leave him. But, then, he made it easy at the last. I was in the process of filing for divorce when he was killed in a car accident. The night I left I determined never to see the man again. As it turned out I did see him one more time. My lawyer contacted me when he was killed and I identified the body. I paid off the lawyer and left town. Fortunately I had enough to live on until this job with Silco came along. And that, Simon Kendrick, is that. Clear?"

"Very," he agreed dryly, leaning casually against the refrigerator again and gazing down blandly into her angry, upturned face. "I'm sorry, though, Kirsten, but I can't let it rest there. Why did you hate the man so much? In fact, why did you marry him in the first place?"

"None of your damn business!"

"Honey, everything about you is my business." Without another word he stepped over to the garbage can and retrieved the letter from the box.

"Read it," he said softly, handing it to her.

Kirsten shook her head mutinously, refusing to take it from him.

"Take it, Kirsten. I want all the ghosts put to rest." It was a command, clear and simple. And she wasn't going to obey it for the world.

"Kirsten, I never bluff. That means I never give orders I can't enforce. Don't make me force you."

"That's exactly what you're trying to do!" she ground out. "I won't be bullied! You Marines are all alike and I've had it with the lot of you! Get out of my kitchen and out of my apartment. Now!" Kirsten hoisted the skillet threateningly and was immediately sorry as Simon's right hand flashed out, disarming her instantly.

"Stop behaving like a child," he ordered, setting the pan down firmly on the counter and pushing the letter into her numb hand. "Open it," he grated, standing over her in a menacing manner that made her sorry she hadn't struck him while she'd had the chance. But, then again, with his thick skin the skillet probably would only have bounced off, leaving him undented, she thought furiously.

Kirsten glared at him, knowing herself helpless and hating the feeling more than she'd hated anything else in the world except Jim Talbot. But she knew there was not one damn thing she could do to change the situation short of running, screaming, out into the parking lot. She was, Kirsten decided, a victim of her size and lack of self-defense training. Someday, she promised herself as her fingers ripped open the letter with a vicious gesture, she was going to remedy that last matter. Trembling with fury, she read the note in her late husband's handwriting.

Dear Kirsten:
I know you'll be coming home when you've had a chance to calm down. Like most women, you're too emotional for your own good. Unfortunately, there's a chance I won't be waiting in the doorway to greet my errant bride. If that's the case, you'll be reading this letter instead. I'm going to the cabin for a few days until the atmosphere settles. When you return I want you to wait two weeks for me. If I haven't put in an appearance by then, take the Heart and the lighter to Phil Hagood. He's never met you but he'll

59

recognize the medal and the old Zippo. Tell him to remember me occasionally when he uses the lighter. Will you think of me once in a while, also?

It was signed, simply, Jim.

"Who's Phil Hagood?" Simon had been reading over her shoulder.

"A buddy from Vietnam, I think. Jim used to keep his address handy." Kirsten's surprise at the strange letter had cooled some of her anger. She reread it quickly and this time shook her head in exasperation.

"The personality of Jim Talbot is totally summed up in that first sentence," Kirsten told Simon dryly, tapping the letter with one finger. "The man actually had the gall to think I'd come back to him!"

"What exactly did he do to you, Kirsten?" Simon pushed gently, curious eyes intently studying her thoughtfully bent head.

Kirsten sighed and slanted a resentful glance up at him. Having lost the main battle, there didn't seem to be any reason not to give up the minor skirmishes, too. At least for now.

"I met Jim Talbot, correction, Lieutenant James Talbot, USMC, six months ago. He was no longer in the Marines, you understand, but a Marine never forgets. Or is that an elephant? At any rate, I made, as I stated earlier, the biggest mistake of my life and thought he was what I wanted for a husband. I was assisted in that decision by the fact that my father, also an ex-Marine, thought Jim was terrific. I now realize that having worn the uniform, the man could do no wrong in Dad's eyes. For some idiotic reason, I considered my father a good judge of men. Jim and I were married within a month. He began playing around almost immediately. I guess it would be more accurate to say he had never stopped playing around. I was pleased to make the discovery because it gave me the excuse I had been looking for since the first week of my marriage to leave."

Kirsten paused to see how Simon was taking the narrative. He was back to lounging against the refrigerator, she noticed. His expression was attentive but blank. Drawing a breath, she continued.

"I had found myself married to a man incapable of really caring for others. A wife was a convenience, a toy. In my case she was also the daughter of a World War II lieutenant colonel who was awarded the Navy Cross for valor in action. The Marines were the only thing Jim had ever cared about. The idea of marrying 'in the family,' so to speak, intrigued him for a while. For my part I was quite dazzled. He was witty, charming, intelligent, and my father approved completely. Also, as you, yourself, mentioned this morning, I wasn't getting any younger and it didn't look like the great love of my life would ever appear. I decided to settle for a romance that I could nourish into something stronger. I reminded myself of all those tales one hears of love growing after the wedding. But nothing grew after this marriage. Just the opposite. Things fell apart quite rapidly. Then I made the discovery that Jim was seeing another woman and I told him very calmly that I was going to file for divorce. It was then I discovered that, in addition to his other attributes, Jim Talbot could be a very brutal man."

"What happened, Kirsten?" Simon prodded in his deep, patient voice.

With a start, Kirsten realized she was no longer seeing the big man leaning against her refrigerator. She wasn't seeing anything in her kitchen, for that matter. Instead, she was in another town, reliving another event in a different apartment.

"He beat me," she whispered. "So badly I thought he would kill me."

She heard Simon draw in his breath with a small, harsh sound and refocused her gaze on him. Lifting her head proudly, she finished the story.

"That's the whole tale. Our little confrontation occurred late one night after he had returned from a date. He'd had a few drinks and I probably should have had the sense to face him in the morning. But I wanted out! I got out, all right. In fact, I was unconscious." She smiled with bitter self-mockery.

"When I awoke he had passed out on the bed. I grabbed my purse, the keys to my car, and made it to a hotel several miles away before I collapsed. The next morning I phoned a lawyer friend and had her start the divorce action. I never saw Jim alive again. The rest you know. He was killed a week later and I did my best to put the whole mess behind me. I only went back to the apartment on one occasion in order to collect my clothes and pay some bills." Kirsten nodded toward the shoebox. "That hadn't arrived yet and I suppose it's been following me around ever since."

With what she privately felt to be an amazing example of self-control, Kirsten pulled herself together and glared at Simon. "Well? Now you know the entire sordid story. Aren't you appalled to discover that the woman you decided you 'wanted,' at least for this week, is trampling on the honored memory of an ex-Marine?"

"Hush, Kirsten," he whispered, straightening and coming toward her in one large stride. "It's all over now," he added, folding her back into his giant embrace and rocking her gently as if she were a child. "You did the right things all along, you know. You acknowledged the mistake of marrying Talbot and you got out. There's no reason in the world why you should feel obliged to limit your social life out of respect for the dead. Especially when the dead doesn't deserve it. Building a new life is much more important than remembering an old one that was a disaster from the first!"

Kirsten stood stiffly in his arms and listened as he talked softly. How much of this comfort was real, she wondered dismally, and how much was prompted by his desire for her?

"You're not the only one to make the mistake of marrying the wrong person, honey. Hell, I did the same damn fool thing when I was twenty-nine. A full-grown man who should have known better. Someday I'll tell you all about it. Now all I can say is that I'm sorry Jim Talbot is dead. It would have been such a pleasure to have bashed in his head!" Simon concluded with great feeling.

Kirsten, who had been perilously close to tears, suddenly found herself unable to contain a burst of laughter.

"What's so funny?" Simon demanded, pulling back to get a look at her face.

"The thought of you bashing Jim Talbot! A typical Marine approach to the situation! Still, it might have been interesting to see him try and talk you out of beating him up on the grounds that you had both been comrades in arms! He was big, too, but not quite as large as you. You probably could have crunched him, but, then again, maybe not. He used to be proud of the fact that he didn't mind fighting dirty!"

"What Marine isn't?" Simon smiled smoothly, one large finger flicking the hint of a tear away from the corner of her overly bright eye. The silver of the hook gleamed for a moment in the morning sun as he lowered his arms.

Kirsten shook her head, grimly aware that she never would understand the male approach to life. At least, not the approach of very large, macho types such as ex-Marines!

"So Talbot put a lot of stock in the fact that he had been a Marine, did he?" Simon went on musingly, apparently unaware of Kirsten's disgust.

"I think his time in the service was the only thing that ever meant anything at all to him," she sighed. "All of his other emotions seemed superficial, almost falsely dramatic, like that hint in the letter that he might not ever see me again. But he really did care about the Marines." Kirsten tossed one braid back over a shoulder, amazed to find some of her earlier resentment against Simon disappearing. He was the first person she had ever told about Jim Talbot and, after the past months of silence, it was a relief to talk it out. Even her father had never heard the full story.

"Are you ready to eat now that you've completed the inquisition?" she asked on a carefully flippant note.

"I'm starving. In all fairness I ought to warn you that I didn't get this size from eating a slice of toast and a cup of coffee in the mornings, which is probably what you subsist on," Simon responded lightly, a crooked little smile touching his mouth. It was astounding, Kirsten thought inconsequentially, how many of his smiles actually did reach his eyes. Yesterday she had been quite certain none of them ever did.

"Is that a hint that I'm supposed to use a couple of extra eggs in the omelets?" she demanded darkly, grateful to be able to get onto another subject and put the past behind her again.

"Umm. And lots of toast with jam and butter. I'll set the table," he added, opening drawers until he found the one he wanted. "Aha! I thought I remembered seeing the silverware when I was picking up this morning!"

"I—I haven't thanked you for what you did in here." She waved in the general direction of the living room, concentrating on counting out the eggs she needed. "It was nice of you to get some of that stuff off the floor and back where it belonged." It took an effort to thank him, but Kirsten was aware she owed him that much.

"It was the least I could do after making use of your couch last night. Although my back may never be the same," he added reflectively as he set the napkins and glasses on the small round kitchen table, which had been designed to resemble an old-fashioned ice-cream-parlor table.

"You have only yourself to blame," Kirsten began severely as she whipped the eggs furiously.

"But, Kirsten, honey! You made it very plain that I wasn't welcome to share your bed and I didn't care for the idea of sleeping on the floor. . . ." He caught her eye with an expectant look. "Maybe tonight you'll take pity on me and let me try your bed?"

"No!" She flung the eggs into the pan with a savage motion, her softer feelings toward the man evaporating rapidly. "I sleep alone, Simon Kendrick, and will for a long time to come! Besides," she went on spitefully, "if you turned in your sleep, you'd probably crush me to death!"

She was unaware that he had moved up behind her until his hand settled on her small waist. Kirsten continued to watch the omelet as if it were a snake.

"I'd be very, very careful with you, Kirsten," he murmured in a low, roughly textured tone and then he dropped a feather-light kiss on the soft nape of her neck. The sensations it produced made her tremble ever so slightly.

"Excuse me," she said firmly, reaching for a warm plate. "The eggs will be ruined if I don't get them out of the pan soon."

Simon said nothing but she knew he was smiling as he went back to finish setting the table. Overbearing, overconfident, and overwhelming man!

Kirsten served the meal in silence and they ate without much conversation. She was astounded at the amount of food he could consume.

"Have you ever had to watch your weight?" she asked finally as the sixth piece of toast disappeared.

"Never," he stated with satisfaction, deftly buttering a seventh slice single-handedly. "What time does the manager's office open, honey?" he asked, chewing.

"Why?" she retorted suspiciously. She had given up on the idea of trying to make him stop calling her "honey." Two days of knowing Simon Kendrick were enough to make her realize that he tended to do exactly as he wished. Lord! She was going to have to be careful!

"We have to report this little disaster, of course," he said reasonably enough. Then he added blightingly, "Also, I'm going to see if there's a vacancy. Why do you think?" A domineering look challenged her to protest.

"Simon . . ." she began spiritedly, only to be cut off before she could finish the sentence.

"What are you going to do? Move out if I get an apartment next door to you?" He grinned, reaching for his coffee cup. "It's still somewhat of a free country, sweetheart. I can live anywhere I wish. And you're much too feisty to let the thought of me living nearby drive you away!"

"You're absolutely right!" Kirsten retorted, outraged. "I don't intend to move again. But I warn you, Simon Kendrick, if you interfere in my life, invade my privacy, I'll . . ."

"You'll what?" he inquired interestedly, sitting back in his chair.

"I'll call the cops and tell them you're annoying me!" she managed, feeling quite harrassed. Weren't there laws against harrassment? She wished profoundly that the delicately designed chair on which he was sitting would simply give way beneath him.

Simon seemed unimpressed by her threats. Instead he climbed to his feet and began clearing the table.

He was as good as his word, of course. An hour later, after a trip back to the hotel to shave, he was at the manager's office. Kirsten refused to go with him, trying to pretend a complete indifference to the whole matter of where he lived. Irritating man! If only he wasn't so large, she found herself thinking as she made the bed. If he were, say, more the size of Ben Williamson. . . . She tried to imagine sparring with Ben the way she had with Simon this morning. The thought wasn't disagreeable. It would certainly liven up the relationship with the younger man! The comparison, however, reinforced the knowledge of a fact she had been doing her best to ignore lately. Ben Williamson was a very nice, very boring young man!

With a frustrated punch at the pillow, Kirsten wondered why life played such mean tricks. Why couldn't Ben have been just a bit more exciting? Why did high-voltage excitement have to come packaged in such a huge man as Simon Kendrick? With a groan, Kirsten sat down heavily on the bed. Was that what she was feeling around Simon? Excitement? Good grief! Hadn't she learned her lesson? What was the matter with her, anyway?

Never again, she reminded herself firmly. Never again would she trust a man of Simon's size and domineering ways not to use his strength against her! She had to be wary. Surely she had learned from Jim Talbot that such men couldn't be relied upon. The momentary thrills they were capable of generating were a poor substitute for genuine love and affection. And Simon Kendrick was far more dangerous than her first husband, Kirsten realized with a rush of fear. Because never, ever, had she felt the level of excitement with Jim that Simon had made her experience in his arms this morning! Did she really need any more warning than that?

Resolutely Kirsten gave the yellow bedspread one last straightening tug and then went back into the living room to feed her fish.

"You guys certainly weren't a lot of help last night," she accused, lifting the lid of the twenty-gallon tank and watching the fish swim to the surface in conditioned reflex. Obligingly she sprinkled food on the water and observed while they wolfed it down. Greedy little creatures!

"Why didn't you defend the place?" she questioned the two guppies. "You're normally so aggressive." The small, shy glassfish grabbed his food and flashed down through the water to hide in the miniature of a shipwrecked boat.

"Something tells me I'm not even going to get a description from any of you. That's it! Stay uninvolved! Don't you know that's one of the chief social diseases of the age?" The door opened behind her and Kirsten dropped the tank lid, feeling like a fool. Simon stood there grinning.

"Some people talk to plants, I've got a woman who talks to fish!"

"They don't talk back!" she snapped, feeling herself redden slightly.

"Must be dull for you in the evenings," he commented, closing the door behind him. He waved a key in her frowning face.

"It's all settled, honey. I'm two doors down, number twenty-five. Want to help me move out of the hotel? I'll call a furniture rental agency and arrange to have the basics delivered as soon as possible."

"No, I don't want to help you move! Did you think I would?" she said waspishly, regarding him with her hands on her hips, feet apart.

"I think," he said, enunciating clearly, "that you had better stop acting like a spoiled brat." He came to a halt in front of her, the smile gone from his mouth and his eyes.

"What will you do if I don't behave as you wish me to, Simon?" she asked evenly. "Hit me? Beat me?"

"No, I've got other methods," he replied steadily, watching her face.

"Such as?"

"Push me too hard and you'll find out, honey." The smile reappeared. "I know that's a challenge you'll probably find impossible to resist eventually, but I don't think you have quite enough nerve at the moment." He picked up his coat and the shoebox and walked back to the door. "If I'm going to have to do the job myself, I'd better get started. I'll see you later, Kirsten."

"Hey! Wait a minute! What do you want with that shoebox? I told you I was going to toss it out!" Kirsten exclaimed, alarmed.

"Consider it tossed, honey." Then he was gone.

Kirsten stood in the middle of the living room, fuming, for a long moment and then threw up her hands in disgust.

She didn't see him much during the weekend. Occasionally he'd wave cheerfully as he carted boxes in from the back of the Mercedes and once he invited her over for a cup of coffee after the furniture had arrived from the rental store. She accepted warily, but the conversation was only of casual things such as the hassles of moving. Neither one seemed anxious to start an argument. Simon didn't abandon his proprietary air toward her, but at least he didn't attempt to monopolize her for the whole weekend, Kirsten thought grudgingly.

She didn't see Ben Williamson during the weekend. On Monday, when she caught a glimpse of his blond head bent over the equally blond head of the new secretary, Kirsten had the feeling she was going to have to look elsewhere for male companionship. She watched Ben and Joyce studying a document together and decided they would probably make a good couple. This magnanimous feeling lasted for about an hour: the length of time it took for the new gossip to spread through the halls of Silco.

It wasn't that she missed Ben, Kirsten told herself as she went alone to her coffee break for the first time in weeks, it was simply that it was uncomfortable being the cause of so many speculative looks. Against her will she found herself almost wishing Simon's huge frame would appear in the cafeteria and stride over to sit beside her. Wishful

68

thinking, of course. It was well known the man seldom took coffee breaks.

"Well, hello, Kirsten. All alone this morning?" Liz Wilford's dulcet tones interrupted Kirsten's thoughts and she glanced up to see the voluptuous redhead standing beside her table.

"Hello, Liz. How was your weekend?" Kirsten couldn't think of anything else to say. She had absolutely nothing in common with the younger woman.

"*My* weekend was wonderful! Roger took me out on the boat. I gather yours wasn't quite so enjoyable?" The green eyes slid over to the corner where Ben and his new friend sat close together.

"I got a lot done," Kirsten lied, refusing to follow the other woman's glance. "It's so easy to get behind on the housecleaning when you're working, isn't it?"

Liz lifted one shoulder dismissingly. "First things first, I always say. If that's what's most important to you . . ." She let the sentence end on a suggestive note. "But then Ben does sometimes seem a bit young for his age, doesn't he? All that endless talk about sports. I don't know how you tolerated it so long, Kirsten!"

"He's a nice person, Liz." Kirsten found herself defending her former escort in forceful tones.

"Oh, I don't doubt that, but I can certainly understand that a woman might want something more in a man. Roger, for example, has a much wider range of interests than poor Ben."

"Really?" Kirsten let the disinterest show in her voice and lifted her cup of coffee for another sip. It wasn't as strong as the thick brew Simon had made for her on Sunday when he had invited her over for a brief inspection of his newly furnished apartment. Now where had that thought come from?

"Really," Liz Wilford affirmed and then smiled a languid good-bye.

"Annoying woman," Kirsten muttered to herself and finished the coffee with a quick gulp.

When she lunched in the cafeteria on Tuesday, Kirsten made a point of stopping by the small table where Ben

69

and Joyce were ensconsed. She chatted brightly, determined to show that none of the three who were generating gossip had the least worry about it. It was true Ben's brown eyes mirrored a small flash of guilt but it died quickly as Kirsten smiled engagingly down at the couple.

"Has Ben been able to settle your fears concerning the nuclear business?" she asked Joyce cheerfully before walking on to another table. She would be lunching alone again. Simon usually spent his noon meals in conferences, so he wouldn't be coming around to bother her. She should be grateful!

"Oh, yes," Joyce Osborne laughed charmingly, happy blue eyes smiling at Kirsten. A nice girl. "He's explaining everything to me. I was a little nervous, you know," she went on confidentially. "But there seem to be so many backup systems in those plants that I don't see how anything serious could ever go wrong!"

Nothing could go wrong! Kirsten hid a grimace. Didn't the girl realize that the nuclear plants were machines designed by humans, built by humans, and run by humans and that therefore the possibility of human error was always present? Still, she was hardly in a position to be critical of the industry. It was paying her a rather hefty salary, Kirsten reflected with self-derision.

"I'm glad you're feeling better about it. Ben knows a great deal about the subject and should be able to explain it well," she replied, feeling very virtuous for giving her former dating partner such a nice pat on the back. She could see him preening under it.

"Thanks, Kirsten!" he chuckled. "You know, Joyce and I are discovering we have a lot in common! She wants to learn to water ski and I'm going to teach her. And she's a great basketball fan!" he added with an admiring look at his new girl friend. Joyce blushed attractively and Kirsten felt as if she were intruding on two teenagers in the throes of first love. Time to make a dignified exit. A basketball fan, she thought wryly. Never in a million years could she have worked up an interest in basketball.

"Well, I'll see you two later," she excused herself easily, and with another smile, went to her table to eat lunch. She was pleased that the small exchange had not gone unnoticed by the crowd in the cafeteria. A first step toward putting the gossip to rest, she thought bracingly.

By Wednesday morning, Kirsten was seriously wondering if she shouldn't consider returning to the world of academic librarianship. The world she had left to marry Jim Talbot. The termination of what she had to admit had been a dull little relationship with Ben Williamson and the fears that Simon Kendrick produced in her were combining to throw life in Richland into sharper perspective. Not a single man had walked into the library this week, she told herself, whom she could honestly say she wanted to get to know better. Unable to pinpoint the source of her restlessness, Kirsten decided it had to do with the fact that she simply didn't feel at home in a community where what passed for intelligent conversation tended to revolve around the evils of environmentalists and the wonders of nuclear power. Sports was the chief topic when talk went into a lighter vein.

A boomtown, she thought, depressed. A genuine boomtown. The energy industry dominated the life of the highly transient population of engineers and craftspeople and it was only to be expected that the pace of life was not conducive to the more reflective mode of living she had known elsewhere. But was she really giving the place and the people a chance? After all, outside of Ben, she hadn't really dated. And Simon Kendrick couldn't exactly be described as typical of the average engineer. No, she needed to find someone in the middle ground. A man of intelligence who had a civilized approach to life.

She was in the middle of a phone call to apprise an engineer of the availability of a particular government standard on piping when she looked up from the notes on her desk to see Roger Townsend enter the room. Somewhere in her mind a curious little question arose. Townsend had never sought out the services of the library before.

"Good morning, Kirsten. Thought I'd take a few minutes to get in some casual reading." He nodded his well-groomed dark head toward the file of current engineering magazines she kept in the corner. "I've been so swamped since Kendrick arrived and started yelling for reports and figures that I've gotten behind on my professional reading."

"Help yourself. The back issues are filed over there." Kirsten indicated another shelf nearby. He nodded, and settled himself near the rack. With a last, curious glance in his direction, Kirsten went back to work.

Half an hour later Roger stretched, tossed a magazine aside, and got to his feet to stroll over to her desk.

"I was about to escape to the cafeteria for a cup of coffee. Care to join me?" he invited, smiling charmingly.

Kirsten regarded the smoothly styled hair, the absolutely right coat, and the casually elegant frames of Roger's glasses and returned the smile. Didn't this man represent the middle ground she had told herself she wanted to try? But why was he asking her to coffee? What had become of the slinky Liz? Still, it would be pleasant to share her coffee break again.

"Sounds great," she agreed with abrupt decision. What did she have to lose? At least it would change the subject matter of the gossip slightly. Kirsten wondered what people would make of the situation. Would the news get back to Simon? That wasn't such a humorous thought. It was true she hadn't seen much of the man during the past few days because he was spending long hours at the office. She was often in bed before she heard the Mercedes in the parking lot at night. But she didn't have the impression he had forgotten her either. Only that he was putting his business with her aside while he dealt with other matters. It was disturbing to realize that one could be shelved until it was more convenient, Kirsten thought grimly as she walked with Roger to the cafeteria.

It was also disturbing to be pumped for information, she decided gloomily as she stirred cream into her coffee several minutes later and listened to Roger introduce Simon Kendrick ever so gently into the conversation.

"The man moves fast, doesn't he? He's already dating the librarian after being at Silco for one week! I have to admit that until I saw you Friday night I hadn't realized what that prim hairdo and those businesslike clothes were hiding." Very white teeth flashed in a very engaging smile. Kirsten forced a response, not bothering to correct him on the matter of who she had been with Friday night. If the office gossip was now saying her date had been with Simon instead of Ben, so what?

"Perhaps his ability to see beyond the obvious is the reason Silco hired him," she suggested with false charm. She had to hand it to him, Townsend took the setdown well.

"I'm always willing to learn from a professional," Roger grinned, unabashed.

Kirsten said nothing, contenting herself with a sip of coffee. Where was all this leading?

"A lot of jobs around here could depend on what Kendrick comes up with in the way of recommendations. You know he's only hired for a short time. He's really a consultant, although management would like him to make the position permanent. He's got other interests, I understand, down in California. Nothing to lose by making sweeping suggestions that could get a lot of folks thrown out on their ears!" Roger smiled again. Kirsten was coming to the conclusion she didn't care for his teeth. "How's your sense of company loyalty, Miss Librarian?"

"Why do you ask, Roger?"

"It occurred to me that you might be in a position to learn a few interesting facts over the next few weeks. . . ."

"I doubt it. You're mistaken about the situation. I don't intend to date the man," Kristen announced firmly, her delicate mouth straightening at the corners.

"Hey, I never said you were! But would you actually refuse if he asked you out?" Roger demanded with a frown. Probably couldn't believe any woman would turn down a date with someone as influential as Simon, Kirsten thought with an inner smile.

"That's my business, Roger," she told him gently.

"You're absolutely right," he agreed instantly. "Please forget I said anything at all. In the meantime, if he hasn't already got the inside track, would you consider going out with me Friday evening?"

Vastly surprised, Kirsten said the first thing that came into her head.

73

"Why?" she demanded baldly and immediately felt foolish. What a thing to say to someone who has just asked you out!

"Let's say because I'm learning to appreciate subtlety, Kirsten," he said softly.

The middle ground, Kirsten reminded herself determinedly.

"All right, Roger."

CHAPTER FIVE

Kirsten received the call from Simon's secretary about an hour after her coffee break with Roger Townsend. Emotionally she prepared herself to handle a lecture on the subject of dating Townsend, a subject she knew from experience could easily have found it's way all over the company by now, office gossip being what it was. She had to make a drastic readjustment when it became obvious that Simon had summoned her to his office on business.

"Sit down, Kirsten," he instructed with an absent gesture toward one of the plush seats. His tone was so cool, she decided he must be one of those people who turns on an "office personality" immediately upon arriving at work. He seemed the same aloof stranger she had faced last Friday. If he intended to go through the same intimidation routine, she decided she would walk out and leave instructions with his secretary to call her when he was ready to talk. But to her surprise, he got right down to business.

"I've had a chance to go over the report you left with me and I'm impressed," he stated simply.

Kirsten was startled. This was praise indeed coming from a manager like Simon! His approach made the situation easy for her. She stepped automatically into her "professional personality," too.

"I'll be happy to elaborate on any of those figures. The

report was only a summary, of course. I knew you'd be too busy to go into much detail at first."

He nodded. "You're right. I've been swamped this week. It was a pleasure to read something concise and to the point after wading through all this garbage!" he added with a look of exasperation as he glanced at the piles of paper littering his desk. "You have a flair for business writing," he added admiringly.

"I imagine people want to impress you with the necessity of maintaining or expanding their present budget levels," Kirsten suggested dryly.

"It could be deliberate," Simon said thoughtfully. "Or it could be that most engineers don't ever learn to write very well!"

Kirsten tried to stifle a grin and failed. "Harsh words from a fellow engineer," she pointed out. A now familiar gleam appeared in the hazel eyes, which regarded her blandly across the desk. Simon's left arm moved slightly, drawing her attention briefly to the fact that he no longer seemed to worry about keeping the hook out of sight when she was around.

"I make an effort to be truthful," he noted, watching her with more concentration than the comment warranted. "I appreciate the same effort on the part of others."

"Are you frequently disappointed?" she inquired politely, fighting down a certain nervousness. Why should she be worried? She hadn't lied to this man!

"Rarely. I said I appreciate the effort. I don't necessarily expect it from everyone." Simon paused significantly, one heavy brow quirking upward. "There are some people, of course, who couldn't lie successfully no matter how hard they tried. Such people are better off sticking to the truth. So much less embarrassing for them in the long run. Getting back to your report," he continued smoothly, handing it to her across the desk, "I'd like a bit more information on the cost benefits of the microfilm part of the collection. Can you give me a breakdown on what it would cost to meet our needs with hard copy?" When Kirsten nodded, her mind still on his remark about lying, he added, "Good. I'm convinced, by the way, of the value of having a research expert on the staff, so the library will be assured a place in the new budget. All I want now is to decide whether or not it's necessary to renew those expensive microfilm subscriptions."

"I'll pull the information together this afternoon," Kirsten stated matter-of-factly, starting to rise. Her job seemed secure now, for what it was worth.

"One more thing, Kirsten," Simon announced abruptly, motioning her back into the chair. "I understand you had coffee with Townsend this morning?"

So this was where the comments on the futility of certain people attempting to lie had really been leading, she thought grimly, sinking slowly back into the red chair.

"So?" She hated the defensive sound of the single word, but couldn't control it.

"So I consider it my responsibility to warn you not to encourage the man. He's slick and potentially dangerous." Simon's voice carried no hint that he cared personally about her relationship with Townsend. His attitude was one of a worldly male giving advice to a too-sheltered female. Kirsten was instantly infuriated.

"I'm old enough to make those kinds of decisions for myself," she said aloofly. "In fact, you've already remarked on my advancing years, if you'll recall," she added rather nastily.

"No one, unfortunately, is ever too old to take stupid risks when trying to prove something to another person," he replied wryly, settling back in his oversized chair and thrusting his muscular legs straight out under the desk. The knowing gaze observed her rising color and he shook his head sadly.

"I am not trying to prove anything, especially not to you! Why should I bother?" Kirsten demanded, launching instantly into her own defense. But his words had bitten deep. Was that what she was doing by accepting Roger's invitation? Trying to show Simon Kendrick he couldn't order her life? If she was honest with herself, she admitted, dismayed, she had to admit she had been fairly certain the gossip would eventually reach Simon. True, she hadn't expected it to happen so fast, but it was inevitable. What

77

about her fine decision to try the "middle ground" this morning? Surely that was her real reason? But even as the thoughts flew about in her head, she knew she would ultimately have to face the truth. She certainly wouldn't have to acknowledge it to this man, however!

"Kirsten," he began, almost gently, for him.

"I don't wish to hear any more. I'm glad you're pleased with my report and I will get the other details for you as soon as possible. Now, if that's all you wanted . . ." She stood gracefully to her feet, head high, eyes tauntingly cool. She would not let him intimidate her, she vowed.

"Kirsten!" This time he snapped her name out in such a tone of command that she hesitated in spite of herself. She turned reluctantly to face him, one hand on the doorknob. He was no longer lounging, but sitting forward, his whole body alert and ready to pounce. Kirsten had to remind herself she was safely in an office where her screams would bring hundreds of people within seconds. He hadn't even gotten out of the chair and she felt incredibly menaced! He was like a huge jungle cat sitting there poised.

"I don't want you going out with Townsend, is that clear?"

"You forget yourself, *Captain* Kendrick," she got out in a voice tight with fury. Fury at herself for feeling so threatened. "Silco may remind you of the military world, but there are distinct differences. The chief one being that I'm free to walk out the door any time I choose! Yes, your words are quite clear, but I have no intention of obeying them!" she challenged with a boldness born out of desperation. "What do you intend to do? Court-martial me?"

It was good to know, a part of her whispered, that even when facing such a very large and dominating male she could still give as good as she got. Talbot hadn't completely destroyed her spirit! But he had made her aware of the merit of being cautious, a small, honest voice noted. Her frantic grip on the doorknob testified to that! Had she gone too far?

Simon studied the rigid stance of her slender figure and the storms swirling in the wide gray eyes a moment before saying very softly, "Kirsten, I never give orders I'm not prepared to back up. You may get away with dating Townsend once, but you'll never get a second opportunity. You may not like my method of handling the situation, so think twice before you risk it. I never bluff. Why don't you just relax and give our relationship a chance before pushing too hard?" The gentle eyes appeared too calm as he looked at her, but Kirsten told herself it was only her imagination that made them seem softer. "I'm trying my best to give you time, Kirsten," Simon went on coaxingly. "Don't force me to surrender all my good intentions."

"Good intentions! What good intentions?" she blazed wildly and then fled with as much dignity as she could summon, her emotions in a state of confusion such as she had never known. How dare he presume so much? She would not be dictated to, she swore silently. And she would go out with Roger! It would be a pleasure to spend an evening with a *gentleman*!

That evening around seven o'clock she heard Simon's peremptory knock on her door. She knew it was him. It had the ring of metal and she realized he'd used the hook. Disgusted because she was up to her elbows in aquarium water and debris, convinced she was a mess, she stalked across the room and flung open the door. Why did it always seem easier to fight one's battles when one felt presentable?

"What is it, Simon?" she asked with a polite formality that didn't come off properly at all. She could tell it didn't by the way his lazily amused look took in her rolled-up shirt sleeves, water-drenched jeans, and the braids pinned to the top of her head.

"I see I've caught you at an awkward moment, but may I come in?" he inquired, shoving one large foot over the threshold.

Kirsten glanced pointedly down at the offending foot and knew she'd never be able to push it back onto the step. Then she deliberately studied his expression with a critical gaze.

"Are you hear to yell at me again?" she demanded.

"Will you let me in if I promise not to raise my voice tonight?" he countered good-humoredly.

"Suit yourself," she finally said with resignation. At least he didn't appear to be in a violent mood. "I'm in the middle of a small project, but you can help," she added, a rather nasty notion occurring to her. After his words earlier in the afternoon, she thought, she should have been much too nervous to have him in the house. But somehow she felt able to cope. Perhaps because it was still light outside, the long Northwest days of spring and summer having gotten underway. A false sense of security, undoubtedly. Still, there were plenty of her neighbors outside taking advantage of the remaining daylight to wash cars and carry out trash. If necessary, a good scream would bring several, she told herself almost cheerfully. Determining to get even for his threats about dating Townsend, she led the way into her kitchen, where several pounds of aquarium gravel were waiting to be washed clean under the faucet.

"All you have to do is pour gravel into that container sitting in the sink and run water over the stuff until it's clean."

Simon eyed the task, taking in the bowl that was serving as temporary quarters for several agitated fish, the stack of aquarium plants waiting to be rinsed and the empty tank sitting on the drainboard. Then, with a decisive nod, he stripped off his rather nice, if somewhat severe, coat, tossed it on the small kitchen table, and extended his right hand toward Kirsten.

"It will be faster if you roll up my sleeve," he told her calmly, waiting interestedly for her reaction.

Without a word she stepped forward, unbuttoned the cuff, and neatly rolled it above his elbow, very aware of him studying her bent head as she attended to the task. The hard, muscled arm surprised her a little.

"You don't look as though you make your living pushing paper," she remarked without thinking and then flushed. Of course, being one-handed, it stood to reason that his right arm would have become quite strong.

"I don't do it full time," he told her, taking advantage of her closeness to slide his fingers deftly under her chin and force her to look up at him.

"Yes, well, the fish are waiting," she reminded him,

feeling distinctly flustered, and took a quick step back out of reach. Somehow, she didn't want to hear the rest of his explanation.

When she had decided to put Simon to work, it hadn't occurred to Kirsten to wonder if having only one hand would hamper him, but now when she did think about it she realized there was nothing to worry about. The situation was well under control. As it always seemed to be around Simon Kendrick, she thought ruefully. She watched admiringly as he swished gravel clean in quick efficient moves.

"I always knew engineers must be good for something," she couldn't help saying rashly as he caught her eye. "I'll have to invite you over the next time I clean the aquarium!"

"I have other talents, too, you know," he told her conversationally.

"Oh? Do you do windows also?" she asked, thinking how he filled her little kitchen until there was barely room to move. As she made the flippant reply Kirsten concentrated on lifting the cleaned aquarium tank, preparing to carry it back into the living room.

"Umm. In a pinch. But I really excel at things like mind-reading."

She hesitated in the doorway, the bulky, damp tank clutched in front of her. "How useful that must be in your profession," she finally said brightly and hurried on into the living room.

"I seldom have to use the talent in my professional world. Most people are obvious enough!" He came to the doorway and watched her set the tank carefully on its stand. When she glanced at him he was wiping his hand dry on a towel. "It comes in handy occasionally around recalcitrant females, however."

"Do I hear another warning coming?" Kirsten asked, pretending to study the way the tank sat on its stand. She made an unnecessary adjustment while waiting tensely for his reply.

"Will you have dinner with me Friday, Kirsten?"

She looked up cautiously. She'd been expecting a lecture, not an invitation. Then Kirsten took a firm grip on herself. This was the moment he had been waiting for. "I'm sorry, Simon, I'm busy Friday night." There, it was out. Now would she get the lecture? The atmosphere tautened between them.

"I had a feeling you would be," Simon smiled mockingly. He started forward, relegating the towel to the counter behind him.

"Simon . . ." She lifted a hand to ward him off as he advanced.

"Saturday night?" he tried. pleasantly, still coming toward her. Kirsten could see the glitter in the shifting color of his eyes and she gulped. Her chin lifted determinedly as she told herself she would not be intimidated.

"I'm planning on being busy Sat-Saturday night, too," she lied breathlessly.

"You see how useful mind-reading can be? I know, for example, that you're lying. Kirsten, you're no good at it, so don't even bother to try. Not with me, at any rate."

Kirsten was as far as she could go, the path of further retreat being blocked by the couch. Simon came to a stop a foot away and stood gazing down at her, an amused expression on his rugged features.

"It's not fair for you to try and overwhelm me like this," she snapped waspishly, frowning darkly up at him.

"I wasn't aware we were playing by anyone's rules but mine," he observed, right hand reaching out to catch her chin and thereby trap her gaze. "Let's try this question and answer session one more time. Will you dine with me Friday?"

"No," Kirsten said very bravely.

"Townsend?"

She nodded mutely, her whole being waiting for his reaction. When it came it was so mild she immediately grew bolder.

"And if I ask you not to date him?" he queried dryly.

She licked her lip and said as determinedly as possible, "I'm going to go out with him, Simon, and that's final!"

"Does your action strike you as having all the earmarks

of a kitten rushing into the lion's den and tweaking the bigger cat's nose?" he asked interestedly.

"Not in the least!" she protested, angered now. "I'd say it's more like one individual human being letting another human being know she will not be ordered about!" No! That wasn't what she meant to say, Kirsten realized abruptly! She wasn't going out with Townsend to teach Simon a lesson! She merely wanted to spend a pleasant evening with an intelligent, civilized man! Didn't she? She bit her lip, distressed and wishing she could recall her words. But as is usually the case with rash words, they had already done their damage.

Simon nodded. "Just what I said. We agree on your motives at any rate, even if we don't describe them the same way. Okay, Kirsten. You can have Friday night to prove your point, but you'll have to be prepared to take the consequences."

"Such as?" she retorted, her stomach tightening.

"Such as the fact that I'm claiming Saturday night."

Not so bad, Kirsten told herself in relief. She wasn't certain what dire threat she had been expecting, but an evening out with Simon didn't seem unduly dangerous now. In fact, Simon didn't appear nearly as menacing as he had this afternoon. It was almost as if he had come to some conclusion. . . . Regally, she nodded her head in acknowledgment of his invitation.

"Good." He accepted what surely was a very small victory with a rather inordinate amount of satisfaction, she thought. Almost as if he'd gotten everything he wanted, instead of just one date. "Now let's finish putting this oversized fish bowl together," he concluded.

Feeling somewhat victorious herself at having salvaged Friday night, Kirsten agreed, wishing her voice didn't carry such an overtone of relief.

Half an hour later they finished filling the tank and she watched as Simon expertly netted the last male guppy.

"Be careful of that gorgeous tail of his," she instructed unnecessarily, "It's his pride and joy!"

Simon tossed her an unfathomable look. "I'm quite ca-

83

pable of handling small things without breaking them," he told her quietly and then flipped the guppy into the tank.

Embarrassed, because she hadn't even been thinking about his one-handedness, Kirsten seized on the first thing that came to mind as a way of apologizing.

"You deserve a reward for washing all that yucky gravel," she said briskly. "Will you have a glass of wine? I've got an interesting bottle that I've been looking for an excuse to open." She headed toward the small pantry where her tiny collection of wine was stored.

Simon was on her heels in an instant. "Sounds great," he announced with more enthusiasm than she had expected. For some reason Kirsten was touched.

When she opened the pantry door he was looking over the top of her head expectantly.

"Behold my wine cellar," she smiled, indicating the small racks with their carefully placed contents. "I was thinking I'd try the California Cabernet Sauvignon from '74," she suggested. "I realize it wouldn't impress someone from California too much, but you have to remember that a lot of labels never make it outside the state."

"I know. You're fortunate in having gotten hold of this one," Simon nodded agreeably, stepping around her to lift the bottle from its rack. "Your wine merchant must have connections!"

"He had a friend smuggle it out of California along with a few other bottles," Kirsten explained, chuckling. With a jolt, she realized that it was pleasant to see Simon so pleased.

"We'll enjoy this, Kirsten," he went on, studying the label. Then he walked over to a kitchen drawer, opened it with his hook, and rummaged around for a corkscrew.

"I thought I remembered replacing this last weekend," he told her, drawing the device forth triumphantly. Holding the bottle in the crook of his left arm, he expertly uncorked it and poured it into the glasses Kirsten set out.

"We can let it breathe while I scrounge some cheese and crackers," she told him.

Two glasses later they were successfully discussing the first thing Kirsten thought they had found in common.

Unashamedly waxing eloquent over wines they had known and loved, she discovered Simon was well ahead of her in knowledge but attributed that to the extra few years of age he had on her. His background on the subject was considerably beyond that of most amateurs and he was well versed in matters of soil and climate, blending methods, and the mysteries of vinification. Kirsten was fascinated. It wasn't until he rose to leave two hours later that she realized she had somehow lost a great deal of ground in her struggle to remain free of the man. She blamed the wine and lateness of the hour for what happened when he stepped close and gathered her into his arms.

His slow, lingering kiss completely sapped her will to escape. She simply stood complacently and allowed herself to enjoy the whole thing. Simon's strong fingers worked their way down her back in a sensuous, massaging pattern until they reached the end of her spine, and then they suddenly applied an irresistible pressure, thrusting her hips against his, arching her back over his left arm. The shock of the close contact rolled through Kirsten like a tidal wave, leaving her sharply aware of his male need and desire, and still she couldn't find the energy to resist. Too much wine, she thought feebly, letting her arms twine upward around his strong neck.

Simon didn't hesitate to take advantage of her lack of effort to free herself, some portion of Kirsten's mind noted. His right arm circled her waist and she was hoisted lightly into the air. Closing her eyes against the momentary giddiness, her next sensation was that of the cushions of the couch beneath her. And then Simon was beside her, his weight sprawled half on top of her and half alongside her slender body. Faint alarms were ringing at the back of her head, but when Simon lifted his mouth from hers to gaze down on her reddened lips and shining eyes, she was clinging to him like a vine to a large, solid tree. A warm and passionate tree, Kirsten reflected, meeting his eyes dazedly. For a few magical moments she completely forgot her fear of his size and strength, finding the feeling of being totally engulfed new and exhilarating beyond her most elaborate fantasies.

Kirsten felt her eyes held in bonds of hazel heat and passion as his hand moved with slow deliberation to the buttons of her shirt. She couldn't resist. It had become overwhelmingly important to satisfy the need raging in the almost-green depths. Because satisfying this huge man was the only way she could satisfy the unfamiliar level of desire welling up inside her own body. It had never been like this with Jim, she realized dimly. She moaned breathlessly as strong, rough fingers undid one button with teasing, probing fingers that slipped briefly inside her shirt and then back out to attend to the next button. Why was he taking so long? Kirsten wondered, straining against him until her legs were caught and held still by his strong thighs.

Then, when Kirsten felt she could stand no more teasing, her small, swelling breasts were free and thrusting against the palm of his hand with an eagerness of their own.

"Touch me, Simon," she said huskily, her whispered words filled with pleading desire that she didn't even recognize in herself.

"How shall I touch you, sweetheart?" he murmured against her lips. "Like this?" He took a nipple between thumb and forefinger and tugged with infinite gentleness. Kirsten gasped and clung more closely.

"Oh, yes," she whispered in a sibilant tone.

"Or this?" he suggested, mouth descending to cover hers as his hand released her breast to trail tantalizingly down to the waistband of her jeans. He let his fingers dip inside and she instinctively sucked in her stomach at his touch.

"Simon!" Kirsten ground out against his lips, opening her teeth and feeling his tongue rush inside.

"What, darling?" he prompted.

"Simon, I don't think I can stand it!" she wailed, a shudder going through her.

"Do you want me, sweetheart?" His mouth moved to her throat and she gave a small cry of joy.

"Yes, Simon. Please!" Was this really her? Kirsten wondered, amazed.

"I'm all yours, honey," he promised soothingly. "But

there's a price tag attached," he added. There was a moment of silence while Kirsten tried to rouse herself enough to understand his meaning.

"Price tag?" she questioned. The alarms in her head sounded louder now.

"Ummm."

"What—what price?" she asked fearfully, a foreboding feeling beginning to push aside the passion of a moment earlier.

"You must surrender to me completely first," he said, his words thick and rough against her throat. "I won't allow you to taunt me with other men, honey. You can't lie with me tonight and then see another man this weekend . . ."

Reality came rippling back, bringing Kirsten out of her passion with a crash. For an instant she stared at him, gray eyes mirroring the fire his words had ignited deep within her just now.

"You did this deliberately!" she accused, struggling to free herself.

"I always make love to a woman deliberately," he agreed, the passion fading quickly from his own eyes. Apparently he had not been as aroused as she, Kirsten thought, and the knowledge angered her further.

"Still going to be busy Friday night, honey?" he whispered coaxingly, right hand stroking her hip.

"Yes!" she blazed. "I'm still dating Roger Friday night! How dare you think you can control me like this with— with . . ."

"With sex? Why shouldn't a man be able to control his woman with sex? Women don't hesitate to use it to keep men in their power."

"Let me go!" she hissed, scrambling out of his embrace and wishing she had something large to use against his mocking, smiling face. He let her go, surprisingly, watching as she rebuttoned her shirt with trembling fingers and thrust the ends back into her jeans. "This was a low, mean, underhanded . . ."

"You look cute with your hair pinned on top of your head like that," he remarked as if he wasn't listening to her at all. "And when you frown like that you look like a little gray-eyed owl!"

"Very romantic! Since you've finished with the lovemaking this evening, will you kindly remove yourself from my apartment?" Kirsten bit out.

He sighed and got slowly, lazily to his feet. He looked barely rumpled, she decided, her fury rising to new heights. How dare he look so neat while she felt totally disheveled! Use sex to control her!

"I get the impression I'm not going to be invited to spend the night," he said with mild amusement. "What's the matter, Kirsten? Is the price too high?"

"Get out!"

"I'm on my way." He started toward the door, snatching up his coat in passing. "One more item," he added, the door open. "Being the soul of honesty that I am, I feel obliged to give you due notice that if you insist on going out with Townsend, matters between us will change considerably."

"Damn it! What's that supposed to mean?" she spat. "That you'll cease favoring me with your *attentions* if I go out with him? Because if it does, I'll enjoy every minute of Friday night to the hilt!"

"No, sweetheart," he grinned wolfishly. "It doesn't mean that at all. It means I shall rescind a few of the female privileges I have been allowing you. We'll start doing things my way." Before Kirsten could find a suitably sharp retort, he was gone.

By Friday night she had passed through a number of emotions but the predominant one was a determination not to be brought to heel as Simon seemed intent on doing. Kirsten no longer even tried to pretend she was going out with Roger Townsend because he seemed a man from the "middle ground." The date had become an exercise to show Simon Kendrick that she would not allow herself to be intimidated. While instinct told her he wouldn't allow the blatant disregard of his wishes to go unnoticed, logic insisted there wasn't all that much he could do about it. After all, she reminded herself with forced cheerfulness, she wasn't married to the man. Which thought was immediately followed by the memory that Simon had never once mentioned marriage. Only a "relationship."

When Roger knocked on her door she greeted him in her most feminine dress, a vivid red number that made her feel almost vampish. This was not a night for yellow. Kirsten could tell the gown met with his approval by the way he ran his eyes over her from head to toe.

"I have the feeling this could be the start of a beautiful friendship," he said, guiding her into the Cadillac.

Kirsten couldn't stop herself from glancing over her shoulder at apartment number twenty-five, but there was no sign her departure was being observed. She heard herself making a polite reply to Roger's comment and set out to enjoy the evening if it killed her!

Things started out well enough, she decided. Roger certainly didn't stint and even took her somewhere else to eat instead of the River Inn. Then they did the rounds of the few nightclubs in town. All the while Kirsten managed to maintain light, bantering, chattering conversation that appeared to be all that Roger required from a date. It wasn't until almost midnight, when they ran into Liz Wilford sharing a table with Simon, that the evening truly turned sour for her.

"Hello, you two. Enjoying yourselves?" Roger greeted Liz and Simon heartily while Kirsten stood stiffly at his side, wishing they had never walked into the River Inn lounge. Damn small towns, anyhow! The meeting didn't seem to faze Roger in the least, his savoir faire rising easily to meet the occasion. But she sensed a tension in him that surprised her.

From the depths of his chair Simon met her eyes, humor edging his mouth. "Good evening, Kirsten. Having fun on your little fling?" His gaze dropped pointedly to the rather daring neckline of the red dress and then returned to her flushed face.

"Yes, thank you," she muttered in a strained tone. What a mess she had gotten herself into! Why hadn't she stayed home tonight and read the latest issue of the tropical fish quarterly that had arrived that day? What was Simon doing with Liz Wilford? Couldn't he see she was only interested in him because of his position with Silco? Perhaps this was why Roger had invited her out tonight. Liz had thrown him over in favor of Simon Kendrick. Well, Kirsten admitted ruefully, it was only what she deserved. After all, hadn't she finally acknowledged the fact that she was using Roger in a way?

"I'm glad the evening is turning out to be a pleasant one," Simon was saying cheerfully. "Remember that when it comes time to pay for it . . ."

"What are you talking about, darling?" Liz crooned, her long-nailed fingers settling on Simon's arm with the same possessiveness they had once rested on Roger's. It didn't appear to bother Townsend.

"Nothing, Liz. A private joke between Kirsten and myself. Shall we dance?" Simon rose to his feet and the woman obediently got to hers. Just before he turned to follow his partner out onto the floor, Simon glanced at Roger, who seemed to flinch slightly.

"Keep in mind our little conversation this afternoon, Roger. I wouldn't want your career at Silco to suffer needlessly." With a casual nod at a stunned Kirsten, he disappeared into the crowd on the dance floor.

"What," breathed Kirsten with a sickening feeling, "was that all about?"

"Your friend Kendrick," Roger growled, "has no compunction about using his position at the company to get what he wants." His hard eyes never left the milling crowd of dancers.

"Did he threaten you, Roger?" Kirsten gulped.

"You could say that," he agreed, turning to meet her anxious eyes. Then he smiled. "Don't worry about it, Kirsten. I'll be all right. Come on now and let's enjoy what's left of the evening, shall we?" He seemed willing to put the incident behind him, but Kirsten was having none of it.

"But, Roger, what did Simon do? What did he say?" she pushed.

Townsend shrugged and, taking her arm, led her toward

the exit. "Only that I was to keep my hands off you tonight."

"But he has no right to tell you what to do with your private life!"

"I know, Kirsten. But when a man like that holds power, he tends to use it for his own ends."

Silently, Kirsten followed her escort out to the car. A man like that, she thought. Was Simon capable of threatening another man over a woman? She knew the answer to that. Yes. A hundred times, yes! She shivered, wondering what to do now.

"I suppose you'd better take me home, Roger," she said in a low voice.

"I will, Kirsten. My home." She didn't like the note of resolution that had entered the man's voice. Roger sounded almost reckless.

"Please, Roger. I don't want to get you into trouble. Simon might do something drastic!" And I don't really want to go home with you, anyway, she added to herself. Ben Williamson had been easy enough to fend off when it came to good-night kisses. She sensed Roger Townsend might be a different proposition.

"Let me worry about Simon!"

"I would prefer to be taken back to my apartment, Roger. I've had a lovely evening. Let's not spoil it by quarreling now," she said more firmly.

"I'll show that bastard!" Roger whispered half under his breath.

"Roger!"

"Don't worry, Kirsten. I promise you I'm going to be a lot better in bed than that arrogant, overconfident . . ."

"Roger! Take me home. At once!" How much had the man had to drink tonight? Kirsten tried to count the cocktails he had ordered at the various places they had visited and came to the conclusion he was probably more than legally drunk. Dutch courage? Did he hate Simon so much he deliberately wanted to defy the man? Was that why he had dated her? Because he thought it would annoy Simon? Or was it the fact that Liz Wilford had shown a distinct preference for the other man? At the moment Kirsten didn't know or care. She wanted to go home.

"We'll stop at my place for a nightcap. Just what you need to put you in the proper mood," Roger told her, pronouncing his words with exaggerated care.

"Mood for what?" she asked, thoroughly irritated. When would Simon get home? Would he be alone?

"Come off it, Kirsten! You're not a little girl anymore, for God's sake! Be good to me and I'll take care of you later!"

"What in the world are you talking about?" she blazed.

"Simple. We'll enjoy ourselves tonight. No need to tell Kendrick, right? What he doesn't know won't hurt me!" Roger chuckled at his own humor. "You can keep seeing him and when you pick up interesting items, you can pass them along to me. He won't be around forever, you know. When he's gone we'll be able to be more open about our little relationship and I'll see you keep your good job at Silco. I'm not without a bit of power myself, you see," he told her, wagging a finger admonishingly in her direction.

"You've had too much to drink, Roger. Either take me home at once or let me out of the car," she said in a furious, almost savage tone of voice.

"That red dress does things for a woman like you. Yeah, I owe Kendrick something for pointing you out to me. . . ." He took one hand off the wheel and reached out to touch her.

"Keep your hands off me!"

Roger's handsome features suddenly took on a vicious cast, which put Kirsten more forcibly in mind of Jim Talbot than Simon had ever done. She didn't stop to think. She wanted out of that car!

"Come back here, you bitch!" he screamed as she threw open the door while the big car slowed for a stop sign.

Kirsten didn't bother to answer, she was too intent on getting safely out of the vehicle with her small bag. The light wrap stayed behind. She was going to miss it if she didn't get indoors in a hurry. But not for the world was she getting back in that Cadillac. Anger and fear made her exit a speedy one. Quickly she started down the street in the opposite direction, reasoning that he wouldn't be able to back up the car and come after her. The traffic was light but sufficient to prevent that sort of maneuver. She needn't have worried; with a screech of rubber her erstwhile date shot away in the night, leaving her alone to try and find a phone booth. A post-winter chill hovered close and Kirsten began walking briskly, her delicate, strapped evening sandals tapping the sidewalk in an impatient staccato.

She discovered a phone one block farther down the street at a service station that was closed for the night. Stepping inside the booth, she closed the door, thus activating the light, and started digging through her purse for change. She was in the process of dropping the money in the slot when she first noticed the dark blue car. At least, it appeared blue. But in the poor light it was difficult to tell. In any event she didn't pay it too much attention, intent on dialing the local cab company. When the dispatcher finally came on the line she learned she was going to have to wait almost forty-five minutes for a cab.

Sighing, Kirsten told the unsympathetic woman on the other end of the line to forget it. She couldn't last that long in the cold night air. Mentally she ran through the list of people she knew who might be home on Friday night and who would be willing to come and fetch her. She tried two women from work, but neither answered. Finally, growing desperate, Kirsten dialed the operator and asked for Simon's new number. In his usual efficient manner he'd had the phone company install a telephone on the previous Monday. In a town of such rapid growth that had been a feat. Probably knew an ex-Marine buddy working at the phone company, Kirsten thought as she listened to the first ring.

There wasn't much chance she'd find him at home. After all, he had still been on the dance floor when Kirsten had last seen Simon. Perhaps he had taken Liz back to his apartment. Or back to hers. The lifting of the receiver on the other end put a stop to her speculations.

"Simon? It's Kirsten. . . ."

"Where the hell are you?" he fairly exploded over the line, his voice so loud she had to hold the phone away from her ear. "You should damn well be home by now. It's after one o'clock!"

"Not everyone considers one o'clock all that late," she shot back, so annoyed she almost forgot why she had called. When she did remember, it struck her that the situation could be rather embarrassing. But freezing to death or having to summon the police for an escort home would be more so!

"For you it is! Especially when you're on a date with Townsend. Now, where are you?"

"Strangely enough, that's what I'm trying to explain! If you'll hush a minute I'll tell you all about it!"

"I'm listening," he informed her grimly.

Kirsten drew a deep breath and took the plunge. "Roger and I had a slight disagreement. . . ." She paused as Simon swore not quite silently. But he managed to restrain himself from further commentary and she continued rapidly, wanting to get the whole thing over. "I hopped out of the car at a stop sign and the cab company says it's going to be forty minutes or so before they can pick me up. That's probably an optimistic estimate, knowing how overworked they are. Anyhow, I was sort of wondering if you . . ."

"Where are you, Kirsten?" he interrupted tersely.

She rattled off the address, turning around in the booth to read the street sign. As she did she saw the blue car again. It was parked on a side street and probably had every reason in the world to be there, but it was late at night and she was alone on the street corner and it made her nervous.

"Simon, I'm not going to hang around this booth. There's a car parked down the street and I think there's someone in it. I'm going to wait on the other side of the gas station. I'll watch for the Mercedes." Without giving him a chance to respond, she hung up the telephone, collected her purse, and stepped out of the booth.

She wasn't all that far from her apartment, Kirsten reflected. Simon should be able to reach her in a few minutes. She knew he'd come immediately. With another glance at the blue car she hurried into the shadows of the opposite side of the station.

She had barely stepped around the corner when she

heard a car's engine switched on. Knowing instinctively it was the blue car's, a small shiver coursed down Kirsten's spine. A shiver not induced by the cold. Worriedly she cast a quick glance up and down the street but nothing looked inviting. It was a commercial section of town with no friendly houses to try. Everything was closed for the night. The penalty of living in small towns!

She circled the gas station, keeping the building between her and the blue car, which could be heard making a sweep down the street. Tensely she waited for the engine noise to disappear in the distance but it didn't. Instead, the driver seemed to come to a stop, make a U-turn, and start back in her direction. Kirsten knew how frightened she was now by the fact that the cold no longer seemed very important. When would Simon get here?

She was standing at a window on the side of the station and took a close look at it. Maybe the place had a burglar alarm she could trigger by breaking the window. The noise would serve to draw the police and perhaps scare off the blue car. Thoughtfully she leaned over to select a rock suitable for hurling through windows, noticing the snags in her dress as she did so. So much for the lovely red vamp gown, Kirsten groaned, as her fingers closed over a nice-sized rock. She was working up her nerve to destroy private property when the sound of another engine, the engine of a car moving at very high speed, stayed her hand. On the chance that it was Simon, Kirsten picked up her skirt and hurried around the corner of the building. Across the drive-through gas lanes she spotted the Mercedes slamming to a stop, and she started running.

Never had the sight of a very large person looked so reassuring. Her fears dropping away in an instant, Kirsten ignored the quietly disappearing blue car. Simon was out of the Mercedes and moving toward her, light glancing from the steel on his left arm. She didn't hesitate. Kirsten hurled herself against him from two feet away, secure in the knowledge that his rocklike strength could absorb the impact easily. His right arm closed around her immediately, crushing her face against the rough warmth of his jacket. She was lifted off her feet without a word, carried

95

swiftly to the comfort of the car, and tossed lightly onto the leather seat.

"Where's the car, Kirsten?" he demanded, briskly chafing her cold arms with his hand.

"I heard it leave as you pulled up," she answered quickly, uncaring now that all danger was past. "Just some rough type out cruising on a Friday night who happened to run into a lone female. Nothing happened, Simon, I'm fine, honest!" It was true. She had been fine since the moment she had reached the shelter of his arms. The realization came unheralded into her mind and it shook her.

"Oh, Simon . . ." she began wonderingly, trying to read his expression, which was so well hidden in the darkness of the car.

"Don't 'oh, Simon' me, Kirsten Mallory," he snapped in a tone of voice he'd never used with her until now. "I've been through hell tonight and I'm not in the mood for any more games! In fact, as I think I once explained to you, I'm much too old for games, period! Tonight we put an end to them!"

CHAPTER SIX

The drive back to the apartment was accomplished in silence. Simon's harsh reaction to the evening's events had immediately destroyed Kirsten's impulse to confess the change in her feelings toward him. As she sat huddled in the far corner of the Mercedes she told herself she was glad he'd interrupted her before she had said something she might have regretted. She wanted to tell him now that he had no business acting as if she were a schoolgirl who had overstayed curfew but couldn't work up the courage to confront him. She sneaked a glance at his hard profile and swallowed her words. But nowhere in all the discomfort she felt was there any sensation of genuine fear such as she had known with Jim Talbot. She was musing on that point when Simon swung the heavy car into the apartment parking lot and stopped the engine with a swift movement.

He was out of the vehicle and opening the door on her side before she could uncurl from the seat and do the job herself.

"Inside, Kirsten," he instructed briefly. "And don't you dare tell me to get lost now that you're safely home," he warned, taking her keys and opening the apartment door. "In fact, it would be an excellent idea if you didn't open your mouth until I give you permission!"

Kirsten lifted her chin in an unconsciously defiant little

97

gesture and swung around to face him as soon as the safety of her own threshold had been achieved. He might have done her a favor this evening but that didn't mean he could talk to her in that tone, she thought grittily. But before she could open her mouth to give voice to her opinion of overbearing males, his right hand shot out and closed over her lips. She regarded him with startled wide eyes across the huge hand silencing her. With a mental effort she quelled the tingle of apprehension he had elicited.

"Listen to me, young woman, and listen good. I've got some personal business to attend to which will take me about twenty minutes. When I'm through I'm coming right back here and we're going to sit down and hash out a few pressing matters. Nod your head if you understand," he ordered, not moving his hand. There was nothing else for Kirsten to do but nod.

"Good. We progress. Now, while I'm gone I want you to take a hot shower and get into some warm clothes. It's a mite chilly outside to be running around in a dress that looks like it belongs on a Las Vegas showgirl, in case you hadn't noticed. Is that clear?" Again she nodded, feebly. He removed his hand, stepped out the door, and closed it firmly behind him. "Lock it, Kirsten," he called and then she heard his footsteps on the walk leading to his apartment.

Kirsten scurried to the window, curiosity about his "personal business" much stronger than her inclination to obey his orders about the hot shower, although she still felt chilled. She felt a lot colder, though, when Simon's door opened and closed and he reappeared with Liz Wilford in tow.

Kirsten's fingers clenched the curtain in sudden anger that evaporated as quickly as it had arisen when she saw how Liz was protesting the dismissal. Simon, Kirsten was elated to see, ignored the other woman's obvious feelings in the matter and calmly stuffed her into the Mercedes. A moment later the big car purred to life and disappeared out of the parking lot.

Simon was right about the shower, Kirsten admitted to herself as she rubbed her limbs vigorously with a thick yellow towel afterward. Then she padded barefoot into the bedroom and chose a fluffy, cuddly robe and her warmest pair of slippers. Her hair, which had been worn down, was sadly wind-tangled and snarled so she spent several minutes pulling a brush through it and finally pinned it on top of her head in a knot. She was adjusting the last pin when Simon's distinctive knock sounded.

She hurried into the living room and opened the door, not yet certain how she intended to deal with him but knowing that the look on his rugged features earlier hadn't anything in common with the viciousness she had seen on Roger Townsend's. For a reason she was not prepared to investigate closely at the moment, the fact reassured her. She was not so naive, however, she acknowledged privately with a small gulp, as to believe the next few minutes were going to be particularly pleasant. Simon might not be about to resort to physical violence but that didn't mean he would be unable to make the full force of his feelings felt!

Kirsten had lined up several carefully casual phrases that could be used to greet the lion and perhaps soothe his temper, but one glance at Simon's face as he crossed through the door and she decided to keep her casual comments to herself. For the moment.

His quick gaze swept from topknot to fluffy slippers and came to rest on her scrubbed face. Without a word she turned and led the way back into the living room.

Uncertainly choosing a seat on the couch where she had made some effort to mend the ripped cushion after the vandalism incident, Kirsten watched Simon stride across the room and take a seat in the largest chair available. Even that sturdy piece sagged slightly as it received his bulk. But of course it didn't have the nerve to collapse under him.

"I'm glad you find the situation amusing, Kirsten," Simon remarked dryly, leaning back to stretch out his long legs. They were still encased in the expensive material of the suit he had worn that evening. The jacket had been discarded, although he still wore the long-sleeved white shirt and tie.

Instantly she wiped the hesitant smile from her face and wondered if Simon had learned his particularly effective method of intimidating people from the Marines. Marines! Her world seemed overflowing with them! Didn't anyone join the Army or the Air Force these days?

"That's better," he remarked, studying her now sober expression. "We'll get along famously if you've learned to curb that tongue of yours so quickly!"

Kirsten resisted the impulse to snap at him, but it took great effort. Instead, she tried to appear composed and regal, imagining herself to be a queen granting an audience to her privateer. One made some allowances for such men when it came to matters of court etiquette because it was well known that they tended to be a very individualistic lot. And one did, after all, owe them some small payment for their services. . . .

"First things first," Simon began with more than a touch of the severe business tone he used so much at work. "Why did you find it necessary to abandon Roger Townsend's car?"

"I asked him to take me home and he insisted on going to his apartment first. I got out at a convenient stop sign," Kirsten said simply, meeting Simon's eyes directly. He nodded.

"The man made a pass at you?" he demanded.

"Probably no more of a pass than you made at Liz Wilford. In fact," she added reflectively, "probably not as effective a pass, since I didn't go home with him as Liz did with you!"

"We are not discussing Liz Wilford. We are discussing you," Simon said very distinctly. "I want to know why Roger Townsend is showing such an interest in you. Did you lead him to believe you would make a pleasant, easy conquest with which to occupy himself on a Friday evening?"

"No!" Simon's scathing comments infuriated Kirsten to the point where she instantly forgot her determination to be regal. She bounded to her feet, small hands bunched into fists at her sides. "If all you're going to do is hurl insults at me, you can get out! Now!"

"Sit down, Kirsten," he said in a quiet tone that brooked no nonsense. In spite of herself, she sat. "There is no indication that Roger Townsend was interested in you until I appeared on the scene. He and Liz seemed quite content with each other, in fact. So why the sudden shift in attention?" He was still leaning back, to all appearances totally relaxed, his hand absently loosening the knot of the tie. But Kirsten wasn't fooled. Simon Kendrick, to her possibly overactive imagination, seemed a large lion now who had only to extend a casual paw in order to keep an irritating kitten in line. And if that kitten continued its bold ways, then a deep growl would sound a warning. Few kittens would dare push beyond the limits implied by those means of control and Kirsten didn't think she was one of them!

"I've told you why I went out with Roger," she mumbled sullenly, not looking at him.

"I'm well aware of your reasons for dating *him*," Simon nodded impatiently. "We'll get to them later. What we're talking about now is why he asked you out."

"Is it so hard to believe that he might simply like me?" she retorted, feeling abused.

"The man doesn't have enough intelligence to appreciate you, little owl."

Kirsten swung her wide-eyed gaze back to him at that. What did Simon mean?

"No, I don't mean to insult your basic feminine attractions, honey," he continued in a lighter tone, "but common sense indicates a man like Townsend rarely does anything without an ulterior motive."

For a full minute Kirsten traded hard looks with him and then Simon gave a small sound of exasperation. "I didn't mean what I said earlier, little owl, about you letting Townsend think you would be another conquest to add to his collection, so unruffle your feathers. I know you wouldn't stoop that low to scare off me." The words were soothing, cajoling, and Kirsten did, indeed, feel as if her feathers were being stroked back into place. Simon, she suspected, knew exactly what he was doing. One minute he was threatening and the next gentling. One was so grateful for the latter that one tended to overlook the former, she thought grimly. Suddenly it was just too difficult to withstand his tactics. Perhaps if the interview had taken place in the morning when she was feeling more fit, she thought with resignation, she might have been able to hold her own. As it was, the hour was too late and Simon was too overwhelming sitting here in her living room as if he had every right.

"Roger thought that if you were interested in me, I might be able to use the . . . association in order to keep tabs on your thoughts about certain Silco employees," she whispered, her eyes on the lighted aquarium. There, now he had his explanation. Would she get one about Liz?

"Certain employees such as himself?" Simon prompted.

"Probably. We never got too far into the matter. I think I remember him promising to take care of me and my job after you were gone. Shortly after that I made my exit. He was drunk, I think," she added, still not looking at him.

Simon growled. "I warned him not to touch you. . . ."

"So I heard! What right did you have to do a thing like that, anyway?" Kirsten demanded, irritated all over again at the recollection. Her eyes flew back to his, surprising an uncompromising hardness there.

"You will learn, honey, that when it comes to you I intend establishing whatever rights I choose. And now that you're almost mine, I don't want another man's hands on you." So matter-of-fact, the words, Kirsten thought in stunned disbelief. Before she could get the angry comeback out of her mouth, however, he was speaking again, leaning back into the chair as if the next part of the interview wasn't going to be as tense.

"Okay, now for the fun part," Simon announced dryly. "Are you ready to admit the truth of why you agreed to go out with Townsend? We've established his motivation in the matter; let's get yours straight, shall we?"

"I've already explained that to you!"

"The truth, Kirsten. Come on, honey. I bet you've already admitted it to yourself, why not to me? You know you'll be uneasy until you do."

"I thought Roger would be a nice, civilized date! That's

102

the sum of the matter!" But Kirsten couldn't bring herself to look at him while she lied. Her eyes switched back to the aquarium. Amazing how calming an influence an aquarium could be in a household, she thought illogically.

"Kirsten, don't try my patience anymore this evening. For both our sakes!" Simon snapped.

What did that mean? Kirsten felt her fingers clasp more tightly together in her lap. Was he really in danger of losing his temper with her? What did she really know about this man, after all? What if he did lose control of himself and decide to use his physical superiority against her? Unable to resist, she turned once again to meet his steady gaze and knew a vast relief at what she saw there. No, there was no viciousness or brutality in that look. Yet. But there was an implacable desire for the truth. Instinctively she knew she wasn't going to get to bed that night until he had his answer.

"When I accepted his invitation I thought it was because I wanted to try dating an-another kind of man," she got out in such low tones it was amazing he could hear her. "But, I guess there was another reason, too. . . ."

"Yes?"

"Deep down I suppose I wanted to let you know you couldn't monopolize me. . . ." she whispered, unable to shift her gaze now that it had meshed with his.

"Wanted to let me know I couldn't monopolize you, Kirsten? Or wanted to see what I would do if you threw down the gauntlet?" he suggested almost gently.

"I . . ." She broke off, not feeling up to agreeing with him out loud, but knowing he spoke the truth. She despised herself for it. What was wrong with her? She would not be a coward about the matter! Why not admit the foolishness of her actions and get it over with? Kirsten took a deep breath.

"A little of each, I think," she said very firmly but very softly. There. It was out. Whatever else she thought herself at the moment, she did not have to include cowardly among the adjectives! The knowledge gave her spirits a small lift and she met Simon's eyes determinedly. Let him make of it what he would!

"So now you're wondering what the next move is, aren't you?" he queried in a tone that gave absolutely no hint about what he was thinking. He must have found her actions incredibly immature, Kirsten realized with an inner grimace. A man like this who was always so straightforward in his dealings with others must find her petty dating game disgusting. It was, she added morosely to herself. She had known almost from the first that she wasn't agreeing to the date with Roger simply because she found the man attractive. She never *had* found him attractive, so why had she pretended to herself that he represented an interesting alternative to Simon?

"Simon," she replied, ignoring his comment on the "next move," "it's getting very late. I'm grateful for the rescue tonight and I admit that you were right and I was wrong. I should never have gone out with Roger Townsend. I would appreciate it if you could bring yourself to overlook my rather childish behavior, forego any further scolding, and let me go to bed." He couldn't have missed the genuine tiredness in her voice, she thought. It was requiring considerable effort for her to keep her tone level.

An unexpected smile lit Simon's expression as he studied the slender, erect little figure she made in her robe and slippers with her hair piled on top of her head. The faint amusement at the corners of his mouth made Kirsten wish she had put on jeans and a shirt.

"But you really don't want me to leave without telling you what's going to happen now that you've ignored my request not to date another man, do you? Just think of how nervous you'll be tonight, wondering about the future, honey. You'll sleep much more soundly when you know what it holds."

"Simon," she began, making an effort to possess herself in patience, "what are you implying?" The gray eyes began to sparkle with warning. She had let him force the truth out of her tonight and that had been unpalatable enough. What more did he expect her to tolerate in the way of punishment?

"I warned you that our relationship would undergo a change if you pushed too hard." His face gave nothing away. "Monday I'll make the arrangements for our marriage. I had originally planned to give you more time, but . . ."

He might as well have said Monday he'd see about picking up the groceries for all the casualness of his words. Kirsten gaped at him, stunned.

"Marriage," she whispered, casting about in her mind for a more brilliant follow-through comment but finding nothing in the least suitable. "Marriage!"

"Don't look so shocked, little one," he smiled. "You've known all along that I want you. And if you squeeze just a bit more honesty out of yourself tonight, you'll admit you want me, too. I thought you learned that much on Wednesday night when you nestled so sweetly in my arms and begged me to touch you," he said ruthlessly. "Would you like me to repeat the lesson?"

"Simon! Please!" The man was no gentleman, Kirsten seethed.

"It's the truth, Kirsten," he insisted.

"Anyone can get carried away occasionally!" she protested desperately, sensing that escape doors were rapidly closing shut in her face.

"Ummm," he agreed readily. "When you're in my bed on a permanent basis you'll be able to get carried away as often as you like," he promised softly, warmth lacing the rich voice in a manner that severely weakened Kirsten's knees. Fortunately she was sitting down, she thought.

"But, Simon," she begged, "why?"

"Why should I marry you instead of simply moving you under my roof? I keep telling you, honey, life's too short to play games. I absolutely refuse to spend another evening such as this; chasing after you every time you take it into your head to get into trouble! I'm hoping that the bonds of matrimony, weak though they may be in this day and age, will give me a little more control over you. At least I'll be assured that you won't get involved with another man while you're wearing my ring!" He sounded so positive!

"How do you know that? What's to stop me from en-

105

couraging another Roger Townsend?" she demanded angrily, feeling much pressured now.

"Your own basic integrity, naturally," he responded, surprised. "You could never deceive me, Kirsten. I've told you that before. Once I have your promise to love, honor, and . . ."

"They took obey out of the wedding service," she hissed, interrupting.

"We'll have it put back in for this event," he assured her evenly. "As I was saying, once I have your promise, I shall be able to relax slightly. I hope!" he concluded with a small grin. "At least I'll have a woman I can trust!"

Flustered, Kirsten tried to come up with a list of reasons why she absolutely could not marry him, but her brain didn't appear to be working well this evening. Too much had happened and she was feeling too low in terms of energy to fight any last-ditch battles. Tomorrow would be soon enough, she told herself.

"Simon," she tried one last time, "I—I don't want you to marry me just because you *want* me in—in bed! I mean, that sort of thing probably wouldn't last long, anyhow, and there you'd be, stuck with a wife . . ." She was beginning to babble, Kirsten thought dismally.

"There are other reasons, honey," he said lightly. "Such as the fact that you have a natural head for business, which will be most useful to have in the family. But the rest of my reasons for marrying you can be discussed at a later date." He got to his feet and strode across the room, cupping his hand behind her neck and hauling Kirsten to her feet in an effortless gesture.

"Now it's time for you to go to bed. I promise we'll get back to this fascinating little discussion tomorrow!" He dropped a quick, hard kiss on her unresisting mouth and then he was gone.

Kirsten went through the routine of getting ready for bed as if she were moving in a dream. She wasn't even aware she had brushed her teeth until she found herself absently replacing the cap of the toothpaste tube. Then she had a bad moment wondering whether she was in the process of removing it or replacing it. A quick check showed the brush was damp so she assumed the latter. Then she made herself pay attention while she removed the contact lenses. It wasn't until she finally tumbled into bed, pulling the yellow sheets up to her chin, that she remembered Simon had never explained Liz Wilford's presence in his apartment that evening. Simon had a lot of explaining to do, she told herself.

It was the sound of knocking on her front door that roused her the next morning. At first she thought it must be Simon coming to tell her he'd changed his mind. She found that thought so painful that she determined to hide her true feelings behind a facade of indifference. He had spoken in anger last night, she reasoned. Of course he'd be upset when he realized what he had done. And it wasn't as if he loved her, she reminded herself gloomily, flinging on a robe and searching madly for a missing slipper. The knock sounded again and she gave up the hunt for the slipper and headed toward the door wearing only one.

"I knew you'd change your mind," she announced in self-righteous tones as she threw open the door.

"Did you now?" smiled the stranger standing on her step. "You must know me better than I do myself!"

"Oh, Lord!" Kirsten gasped, feeling a complete fool. "Who are you?"

"Phil Hagood," the slim, wiry man said cheerfully, taking in the picture she made in her early-morning attire. Kirsten blushed bright red at the thought of her uncombed hair, half-shod feet, and sloppily belted robe.

"Hagood?" She blinked sleepily, trying to think where she'd heard that name recently. Then she remembered. "Jim's friend?" she asked more sharply.

"Right first time. And you, I assume, are Kirsten Talbot?" Vivid blue eyes regarded her interestedly under sandy brows. Straight blond hair had been combed back from his forehead earlier during the morning but had fallen boyishly to one side now. He was about medium height and dressed in jeans and a western shirt opened rakishly at the collar. He might have just come to town from one of the nearby wheat farms.

"Mallory," she corrected automatically.

"Mallory? You aren't my old buddy Jim's wife?" he frowned, obviously perplexed.

"I was married to him," she admitted. "But it was for such a short time that I went back to using my old name after his death." She became aware of the fact that it was chilly outside and her visitor wasn't wearing a coat. It was also rather early to be paying a Saturday-morning call, not even seven-thirty.

"Won't you come in?" she invited, not certain exactly what her social obligations were to the best friend of a man she cared nothing about.

"I'd be delighted." He gave her his charming smile and stepped inside. If he'd been wearing a Stetson hat, he would have tipped it to her, Kirsten thought with a tiny smile. He even had the soft drawl to go with his overall appearance.

"I only got up a minute ago," she said, stating the obvious. "If you'll excuse me, I'll get dressed and join you in the living room." At his nod she zipped back to her bedroom and began tossing on some clothes. Her mind was beginning to function at last as she inserted the contacts and found herself wondering what Simon would say if he'd seen her greeting this stranger at the door a few minutes ago. Some things are better left to the imagination, she decided.

"Can I make you some coffee, Mr. Hagood?" she asked, walking quickly back to the living room and on into the kitchen. "I'm going to have a cup and you're welcome to join me."

"That sounds terrific, ma'am," he affirmed enthusiastically, rising from his perch on the couch and following her. He swung a leg over one of the little ice-cream-parlor table chairs and sat backward in it, watching her make the coffee.

"How did you manage to locate me, Mr. Hagood?" Kirsten asked casually, pouring water into the pot.

"Please call me Phil," he invited earnestly.

"All right, Phil."

"It took some lookin', I can tell you!" he said feelingly.

"First of all, it was some time before I learned Jim had been killed in the car wreck. That was a hell of a shock! I didn't learn about it until a month ago. Then, when I came to see his widow, I couldn't find a trace of her."

"You knew he had married?"

"Oh, yes. Jim wrote to me right after the wedding and told me he'd married the daughter of a lieutenant colonel." Kirsten winced, but Phil Hagood didn't appear to notice. "Jim said you and I would like each other and we'd all have to get together some day. You know how buddies make plans like that. But he also said something else in that letter, ma'am . . ." The sandy-haired young man paused and waited until he had Kirsten's full attention. "He said that if anything ever happened to him, he'd want me to look after his wife."

That did get her full attention. "Really? Jim never said anything to me about asking you to take care of me," she commented, reaching for the coffee cups.

"Well, you know how it is, ma'am," he began, but Kirsten was getting irritated at being constantly referred to as "ma'am."

"Call me Kirsten," she told him.

"Yes, ma'am, I mean, Kirsten. Anyhow, as I was saying, you know how it is. A man doesn't like to put into words everything he might be feeling. I expect Jim didn't want to make a big fuss about the fact that he'd lined up someone to look after his wife in the event something happened . . ."

"Oh, Jim had quite a way with words," Kirsten interrupted calmly. "He never suffered from a shortage of them while I knew him, at any rate." She waited while the automatic coffeemaker dripped its contents into the glass pitcher and then carried it over to the small table.

"Yes, well." Phil was somewhat embarrassed now. Perhaps he was beginning to suspect that all had not been well between Jim and herself. Jim, of course, would never have told him differently. In fact, Jim probably went to his death thinking there wasn't anything seriously wrong with the marriage! He probably deemed it the normal way of

109

things to treat a woman like dirt and then beat her savagely when she told him she wanted out.

"But Jim did mention me to you, didn't he, Kirsten? I mean, you seemed to know my name. . . ."

Kirsten took pity on him. After all, it wasn't his fault if he was merely another dumb Marine.

"Jim mentioned his friendship with you more than once," she told him gently, pouring coffee. "He seemed quite attached to you. The two of you were in Vietnam together, weren't you?"

"Yes, indeed! I was with Jim the day he caught it in that damn rice paddy." Phil shook his head disbelievingly. "All we ever saw were some kids on a water buffalo and the next thing we knew the whole place was fallin' apart!"

Kirsten nodded sympathetically. What could she say? War must be an incredibly traumatic experience. Perhaps it hadn't been all Jim's fault that he had been the way he was.

"When Jim and I got out we decided we'd keep in touch. We didn't always get to see a lot of each other, but we made sure each of us knew where the other was. In case we needed each other, you know." Phil paused to see if she understood the significance of a war friendship. "Occasionally we'd get together to try out a project or something. . . ."

"A project?" Kirsten inquired curiously.

"You know, ma'am." He blushed with apparent embarrassment. "A money-making scheme or something. Never too successful, I can tell you! Then Jim got smart and went into the electronics business. Me, I decided to try my hand at ranching."

"It was nice of you to track me down to make certain I was okay," Kirsten said gently, wanting to steer the conversation in a slightly different direction. The less reminiscing about Jim Talbot, the better.

"My pleasure! 'Course, I didn't know Jim had got himself such a fine-looking woman," he added with a boyish grin. Bright blue eyes danced merrily as she turned her customary shade of blush-red. Compliments had never

110

been so thick on the ground in her life that she had gotten used to handling them properly.

"I don't believe you ever finished telling me exactly how you managed to locate me," she commented, watching him over the rim of the coffee cup.

"Right. Well, as I said, it took a while, but I finally tracked down a friend of yours who knew that your dad lived in Santa Rosa, California. I wasn't sure of your last name, the one you're using now, and neither was this friend of yours. I did a lot of calling before I finally got the right Mallory even after I was able to make sure of the name. Your dad told me you lived here."

"You certainly went to a lot of trouble," Kirsten smiled.

"Well, not the kind of trouble I minded. It became kind of a game, you know? I felt like I had won the prize this morning when I knocked on your door and you answered it lookin' all nice and mussed from sleep!"

The smart-talking Marine was starting to show in this farm boy. "Phil," she began steadily, anxious to get him off the present track of conversation, "I think it's very kind of you to have taken so much time and effort to find me and make certain I'm okay. But as you can see, I'm doing all right. I have a nice job and I've started a new life for myself. So you have no reason to be concerned about me."

"I can see that. But you understand I had to make sure? For Jim's sake?"

"Yes, I understand. Now what will you do? Have you come quite a distance?"

"Nope. I live on the western side of the state, near Seattle. Got a nice place on the coast with a few horses and some cattle. You'll have to come over and see it sometime, huh?" The blue gaze was quite appealing.

"Maybe," she hedged carefully. "Are you going to be in town long?"

"I drove over for the weekend. I'll start back tomorrow, I guess. I've never been to Richland before. Don't suppose you'd like to show me around, would you? I hear there's a lot of those nuclear reactors being built here. I've never seen one close up."

"You haven't missed much," Kirsten commented dryly and then smiled. "If you want to see some, I'll show you how to find them on a map I've got. It's not hard. Just follow the main road out of town going north. You can't miss them! A few have visitors' centers which have displays and mockups that might interest you."

Disappointment welled in those arrestingly blue eyes. "I reckon that'll have to do. I was sort of hopin' we'd get to talk a little about Jim while we took in the sights."

"Phil, I don't like to discuss Jim Talbot," she said quietly.

"I know. It probably hurts too much," he said quickly, patting her hand lightly. "It's been such a short time since his death. I see you couldn't even bear to have many things around that would remind you of him," he added, glancing around the kitchen and into the living room. "I remember he used to keep his collection of swords on one wall and his books on war history filled a couple of bookcases!"

"I didn't bring any of Jim's things with me," Kirsten told him in a determined voice, wishing he'd get the message.

"Nothing at all?" he asked incredulously, turning to look at her curiously. "You must have saved some stuff, though, Kirsten. I mean, being his widow and all and him not having any relatives to speak of. What about his Heart, for instance. Didn't you even keep that? And there was an old lighter. One I gave him, in fact. Used to be he never let those things out of his sight. . . ."

Before Kirsten could answer that one Simon's steel hook struck the door. She knew for certain it was Simon this time. She had only been mistaken earlier because she had been so groggy. This was all she needed to complete her morning, she told herself as she went to greet her possible future husband. At least he held that status until he discovered she was entertaining other ex-Marines before eight o'clock in the morning, she thought wryly.

CHAPTER SEVEN

"Good morning, honey. I'm glad to see you're up bright and early. I've got plans for us today," Simon greeted her cheerfully, pulling her into his arms.

"Simon . . ." Kirsten tried only to be silenced with a kiss. A kiss that indicated he hadn't changed his mind about marrying her, at any rate. She made another attempt when he released her and stepped inside. "Simon, I've got a visitor," she said quickly, backing up as his solid body moved into the apartment.

"A visitor? At this hour? I can't leave you alone for a minute, can I, sweetheart? Who are you entertaining over the breakfast table this morning? Someone very short and frail, I trust!"

"Simon, I'm serious," Kirsten hissed in a whisper, embarrassed in case Phil could overhear.

"Yes, I can see you are. Better introduce myself, hadn't I?" Without further ado he covered the distance to the kitchen and came to a stop in the doorway.

"I'm Simon Kendrick, Kirsten's fiancé, and I think it's only fair to tell you that I make a practice of crunching other men I happen to find at her breakfast table," he announced pleasantly to a startled Phil Hagood.

The other man got to his feet immediately, uncertain how to deal with Simon and glancing at Kirsten for guidance.

"Simon is only teasing you, Phil. Sit down and finish your coffee," she told him with a withering look at an unrepentant Simon. "Can I get you a cup, Simon?" she offered politely.

"Of course you can. It's one of the things I came over for." He lowered himself precariously onto one of the little chairs and faced Phil.

"Phil Hagood, Mr. Kendrick. I was a close friend of Jim Talbot's. Kirsten's husband," Phil noted by way of introduction.

"I'm aware of the bastard," Simon nodded agreeably. "I prefer not to discuss him, however. What are you doing here in Richland, Phil?" The agreeable tone of his voice did nothing to hide the steel reinforcement buried in it. Kirsten turned in time to catch sight of the hook being casually shifted and she knew instinctively that Simon had decided to be deliberately intimidating.

Hagood had whitened at Simon's reference to Jim Talbot but he controlled himself with an effort.

"Jim told me he married, Mr. Kendrick. He asked me to check on Kirsten if anything ever happened to him. Make sure she was getting along okay. You understand?"

"Ummm. Completely. Kirsten, this coffee is weak. Why don't you try adding another measure next time you make it?" Simon smiled blandly at her as she took the one remaining chair at the table.

"Make it yourself if you don't like the way I do it!" she told him unpleasantly, disgusted with his rudeness.

"All right. Starting tomorrow, making the coffee will be my task. It will be convenient if I don't have to walk all the way from my apartment to do it, though, so starting tonight you'll sleep under my roof."

Kirsten stared at him. A man like Simon Kendrick never did anything without a purpose. Why this kind of conversation in front of a total stranger? Baffled, she glared at him.

Before she could figure out an answer Simon was turning to the reddening Phil.

"Now that you've seen Kirsten is safely settled with an-

114

other Marine I expect you'll want to be on your way, won't you?" he inquired outrageously.

"Officer?" Phil asked uneasily and then glanced briefly at the gleaming hook just visible beneath Simon's white cuff. " 'Nam?"

"Right both times. Would Kirsten accept anything less?" Simon asked curiously.

"Simon!" she yelped furiously. "What's gotten into you? You're behaving like a . . . a . . ."

"A Marine?" Simon smiled dangerously at her and unaccountably she decided to shut up. The man was plotting. She had a feeling . . .

"How far have you come, Phil?"

"Drove over from the coast," Phil muttered, looking harassed.

"Last night?" Simon pursued.

Hagood blinked and shook his head negatively. "Got a real early start this morning," he explained briefly. Kirsten took pity on her guest.

"It's been a long drive which he undertook for the sake of his friend, Simon. You can't ask him to leave. . . ."

"Kirsten, honey, go into the bedroom and pack an overnight bag. I thought it might be nice to spend the weekend, or what there is left of it, in Seattle. We'll have to hurry, though, or we'll miss the plane. It's only an hour's flight over to the city. We'll be there by the time the stores open. Now run along like a good girl while I show Mr. Hagood out."

Kirsten stared at him helplessly. But there was no arguing with the man and she knew it instinctively. There were times when it was safe to stand up to him and other times when it was the last thing in the world a sane person would do. Confused and angry, she slammed her coffee cup back onto the saucer and stalked away to the bedroom.

Ten minutes later she heard the front door close and tiptoed carefully back down the hall. Simon smiled benignly and came toward her.

"Finished packing already? Good girl. We'll have to rush."

"Simon, I am not packed and you know it. Why did

you run Phil Hagood out of here? He was only trying to do a good deed." She faced him firmly, sensing that a confrontation was safer now.

"I'm absolutely serious about the packing, woman. If you don't get to it, you'll have to spend the night in Seattle in whatever you've got on at the moment. Which would be a pity considering the restaurant I have in mind. You won't believe the wine list, honey. Enough to make a person drool clear over here in Richland! Now run along. I'll feed those monsters in the aquarium!"

Kirsten hovered a moment longer, trying to decide if she was being teased, while Simon lifted the lid of the fish tank with his hook and dropped a tiny pinch of food into the water. When he glanced up she turned on her heel and fled in the direction of the bedroom.

The scruffy desert surrounding Richland and the neighboring towns of Pasco and Kennewick fell away rapidly as the commuter plane climbed into the sky forty minutes later. They had barely made the flight. The rich farmland of the Yakima Valley was passing underneath before Kirsten had the courage to direct Simon's attention back to Phil Hagood.

"I don't think you should have been so abrupt with him, Simon. He didn't know what the situation had been between Jim and me!"

"The guy's a con artist, Kirsten. There's no point being polite to con artists, honey, it only encourages them," Simon countered smoothly, opening the airline magazine to an article on home computers.

"A con artist! How would you know a thing like that?" she demanded, irritated. "He seemed like a perfectly pleasant farmer type to me. And it was nice of him to go through all that trouble to find me. . . ." Kirsten broke off, remembering something. "I meant to give him Jim's Purple Heart and that lighter. I think Phil's the one person in the world who would care to have them. I got so flustered when you started acting the part of the jealous fiancé that I forgot," she frowned.

"I wasn't acting, sweetheart. Believe it or not, I really

116

do intend to put a stop to this habit you're developing of inviting strange men to breakfast!" he announced dryly, glancing up briefly from his magazine.

"Simon, don't be an idiot!" she snapped. "You're the only other 'strange' man I've had to breakfast in ages. Come to think of it, maybe I should put a stop to the practice," she added musingly. "Look what happened to me after I fed you."

He grinned. "Meeting you has caused a severe interruption in my routine, too, honey! I haven't had a dull moment since I knocked on your door that night after Williamson left!"

"Yes, you looked anything but bored last night with Liz Wilford," Kirsten commented in dulcet tones, turning her widest, most innocent gaze on him.

"Little cat," he said, amused. "It wasn't my fault I was left at loose ends last night. It would have been you dancing with me if you had accepted my invitation instead of electing to get into trouble."

"I wasn't in trouble," Kirsten muttered. "I just got mad at Roger and decided to come home on my own!"

"You mean with a little help from a friend, don't you?"

Kirsten ignored the humorous note in his words, deciding to go on the attack. "I wasn't aware you and Liz were such good friends," she remarked aloofly.

"We aren't. At least, we're not any closer than you and Roger," he told her gently, the laughter lighting up the hazel eyes. "I'm afraid Townsend was trying to cover all bases."

"You mean Liz was supposed to be pumping information out of you, too?" Kirsten thought about that a moment and an irrepressible grin bubbled to the surface. "I resent that!" she exclaimed with mock indignity. "He didn't even give me a chance! I might have made it very successfully as a spy! But if you knew what she was doing, why did you let her wangle the date out of you?"

"I've told you. I had nothing else to do except wait for you to come home. I decided to amuse myself until the time came for me to start calling Townsend's apartment every fifteen minutes," he informed her blandly.

"What! You mean on top of merely threatening the poor man with his job you were going to pester him over the phone, too?" Kirsten demanded, not certain whether to scream or laugh and very much afraid she would do the latter. Simon was so incredibly determined to have things run his way!

"Whatever it took to make sure he kept his hands off you," Simon agreed with a massively indifferent shrug.

"This *relationship* of ours appears to suffer from a lack of personal privacy," she announced feelingly.

"It's not privacy you need, sweetheart, it's something to keep you out of trouble. I'm hoping marriage will do that, but if it doesn't at least I'll be close enough to step in before things get out of hand."

Kirsten shot a quick look at him and then concentrated her gaze on the huge, circular, irrigated fields that dotted the landscape below the plane. "Simon, were you really serious last night?" she asked as softly as the noise of the plane allowed.

"I never say anything I don't mean," he answered simply, flipping to the next article in his magazine.

Kirsten ground her teeth at his casual attitude toward the subject of their marriage. Perhaps he married regularly?

"Simon, are you divorced?" she said quietly, remembering the vague "mistake" he had alluded to the morning she had told him about Jim. She turned a bit in the seat to meet his steady hazel gaze.

"Yes," he said honestly. "But you needn't concern yourself with worries over an ex-wife who may descend on you at any moment. She's completely out of my life and there were no children. Does that satisfy you?"

She stared at him for a long moment, reluctant to put her thought into words but found herself unable to avoid it. Trying to cover the remark with a decidedly flippant note, she said, "It's only that I can't imagine a woman leaving you alone after she'd been married to you."

Simon smiled and reached out his right hand to flick her cheek affectionately. "I told you, honey, the marriage was a mistake. Like you, I had pretty well decided that I was

118

not fated to enjoy a great love in my life. In fact, I had decided that there was no such thing. Sylvia came along right after I had come to that conclusion and she offered everything I thought a rising executive ought to have in a wife. And she did. We managed to live two separate lives under the same roof quite successfully. Then came the day when I decided I no longer wanted to be the rising executive she had married. Our marriage had been something of a business arrangement and, in a sense, I was not holding up my end of the business any longer. We split. No hard feelings on either side."

"But, Simon, you are obviously successful now. Did you change your mind and go back to your original ambitions after the divorce?" Kirsten asked wonderingly, thinking privately that the split between Simon and his ex-wife probably hadn't been quite as smooth as he made it sound.

"Nope," he grinned down at her. "Poor Kirsten! You don't know very much about me, do you? I only do this consulting bit a couple of times a year for short periods to supplement my regular income which, until recently, has been rather limited."

"But the Mercedes, your clothes . . . Simon, you don't look particularly poor," she pointed out, confused.

"Window dressing, sweetheart. I have to maintain an image or I wouldn't get the juicy contracts I've needed." He spoke in a very off-hand fashion. "No one would hire a management consultant who looked as if he needed a job!"

Kirsten giggled, delighted. "Then you're not terribly rich?"

"Most of what I possess is tied up in my land," he smiled, watching her interestedly. "Will it bother you to live in an old stone house in a vineyard in Napa Valley?"

"A vineyard! Simon, you own a winery down in California?" she gasped, entranced. Several facts were falling into place now, she thought.

"A small one, honey. But it's growing. I guess I should tell you that I don't ever intend to let it get very big, because that would kill the uniqueness of the product. Therefore, we probably won't ever be particularly rich." He was watching her intently and whatever he saw in Kirsten's gray eyes must have satisfied him. "I had a feeling the first day I met you that you weren't cut out for the corporate world. Somehow, in my mind, I could visualize you perfectly helping with the harvest!"

"A nice, sturdy peasant type?" she suggested with a laugh and when he responded with his wolf's grin she suddenly decided that, whatever became of Simon's marriage plans for her, she was going to enjoy this weekend! There might be some very excellent reasons not to risk marriage with the man, but she felt unable to deny herself the excitement of his company in Seattle. The future would take care of itself.

Below them the agricultural lands rose into foothills that became the peaks of the Cascades. Off the wing of the craft Mount Rainier thrust some fourteen thousand feet into the clear sky, the glaciers that rimmed its sides glittering in the sunlight. At last the flat lands of eastern Washington had given way to the picture-postcard Washington. Majestic forests, fantastic skiing slopes, and tumbling rivers passed beneath the wings.

"Do you have any idea how many people accept jobs in Richland, sight unseen, thinking they're moving to a Washington that looks like this?" Kirsten smiled up at Simon at one point, indicating the panorama below. "One month shortly before you arrived, Silco had six different people accept an offer to take over the quality assurance department manager's position. All six declined the offer after they came to Richland!"

"The desert didn't drive you away," Simon noted.

"I couldn't afford to be choosy. Silco pays well and I needed the money. Still, I had just about made up my mind to start active job hunting over on the coast when you appeared on the scene."

"Was that why you acted like you couldn't care less if I had you fired?" he inquired silkily.

"That and my own natural perversity, I guess," she admitted ruefully.

"Not about to let any man think he could seriously affect your future emotionally?"

"Right!" she agreed with fervent cheerfulness. "Besides, I think I would be happier getting back into academic librarianship and out of the corporate side of life. . . ." she concluded on a more musing note, thinking of how nice it would be to harvest grapes and make wine for the rest of her life.

"Did you expect to find lots of short, weak men on a university campus?" Simon inquired teasingly.

"You're never going to let me forget that I held your size against you, are you?"

"Never. In fact, I intend to use the disparity in our height and weight to my advantage," he informed her, domineering eyes gleaming through narrowed lids.

"Oh?" she retorted witheringly.

"Ummm. Whenever you get out of hand I shall simply pluck you up, tuck you under my arm, and cart you into the bedroom."

"Simon!" she flushed, horribly afraid the people in the seats ahead might have overheard.

"Yes, honey?" he drawled softly.

"Simon," she began again in a very low, very intense voice. "You do see marriage as a . . . a partnership, don't you? I mean I'm not saying I will marry you, but . . ."

"A partnership's important to you?" he asked speculatively, ignoring her last sentence as if it were irrelevant.

"Oh, yes! I couldn't abide being someone's *thing* again!" she managed huskily. Her eyes never left his face while she waited tensely to see if he understood.

"You would never, ever be my *thing*," he whispered back in an equally intense tone. "But you *will* be my woman. Do you understand the difference?" The probing eyes trapped hers in a steel grip. The man could be steel all over, Kirsten thought. His eyes, his hand . . .

"I think you might be inclined to assume too many rights!" she began heartily, trying to gauge his temper. "The things you said to Phil this morning, for example. Why did you have to act so possessive? He certainly wasn't trying to seduce me!"

"No? There are a variety of approaches when it comes to seduction, Kirsten." Simon's voice had taken on that aloof, instructing tone he could use so effectively at work. She felt her hackles rise. And just five minutes earlier she had been feeling so compliant!

"And you are the expert on the subject, I presume?" she shot back. "What approach did you use on Liz Wilford last night?" Kirsten knew the other woman had not gone home early willingly, regardless of what her initial intentions for the evening had been. She'd had a quick look at Liz's expression as Simon had put her into the front seat of the Mercedes.

"I crooked my little finger and she fell into my arms," he told her with supreme male satisfaction.

"Why, you . . ." Kirsten was forced to forgo her infuriated tirade as the pilot's voice came over the public address system, warning them to fasten their seatbelts in preparation for landing. By the time she could make herself heard again, the moment was lost. She contented herself with a furious little glare and then forgot the argument as they settled in for a landing.

Seattle was living up to its reputation with soft drizzle and a heavy, gray, overcast sky. But no one seemed to mind. Simon took charge in his familiar, efficient way as soon as they landed. In a remarkably short period of time a car had been rented and they were on the freeway into town.

"Haven't you heard there's an energy crisis on?" Kirsten asked, surveying the inside of the large vehicle Simon had chosen.

"In my case it comes down to a choice between respecting the energy crisis or my personal space crisis," he grinned tolerantly, changing lanes expertly.

"Where shall we go first?" he asked twenty minutes later, checking them into a two-room suite in the tall, modern tower of a downtown hotel.

"How about a tour of the lobby," she suggested dryly, taking in her surroundings with awe. She was accustomed to a lesser breed of lodging. "I thought you said you didn't have all that much money."

"Silco is paying well and I figure we deserve it. Think of it as a sort of pre-honeymoon treat!"

"Simon!" Kirsten choked, whirling to confront him as he hooked her overnight bag and started toward the elevator. Either the bellhop had moved too slowly for Simon's liking or her fiancé considered two small flight bags insufficient luggage to warrant acquiring the services of one. She found herself addressing his back, however, so gave up her scene in favor of gaining a place in the same elevator. Simon had given no sign of being willing to wait while she snarled at him in the elegant lobby. Nor could she say anything in the crowded elevator.

Once in their rooms, Kirsten was forced to put off the confrontation over Simon's implicit assumption due to the demands of the enchanting view stretching out below the windows. She would worry about which of the two rooms he planned to use later. To her right Elliott Bay with its crisscrossing ferries dominated the picture, the scene so attractive that she made her decision about where to start touring immediately.

"Let's head for the waterfront," she began excitedly. "We can walk to Pike Place Market from here, according to this map, and then down to the import shops on the piers . . ." She broke off, studying her map again. "And then we can amble on down to Pioneer Square. . . ."

"That's a hell of a lot of ambling," Simon interrupted with a laugh, setting down their bags and crossing the thick carpet to stand beside her at the huge windows. "We could take the car."

"Too much trouble to park," Kirsten shook her head. "No, if we get tired we can try this free bus service," she added enthusiastically.

"All right, honey, on your head be it. I warn you, though, I don't intend to carry you in to dinner if your feet give out! Have you ever been to Seattle before?" he asked, watching her animated expression.

"No. I've been meaning to get over here, but this is the first chance I've had." Kirsten wisely decided not to mention Ben Williamson's offer. "I came from Oregon after Jim's death." She hesitated, wishing she hadn't brought up that subject either. "And there hasn't been much time to do any touring yet. Too busy settling into my new job and Richland."

Walking down to the elaborate farmers' market that had grown from a series of vegetable stalls into a rambling collection of shops, bakeries, fish stands, and cheese shops was easy. Kirsten forgot about the necessity of having to walk back up the hill in the flurry of shopping. They bought packets of aromatic spice tea, gazed longingly at rows of imported cheeses they knew would never survive the trip back to Richland, and dined on Middle Eastern fare. Through it all Simon rarely let go of her hand and she didn't bother to try and free herself.

"You know, you're a great asset in a crowd like this," Kirsten grinned at one point. "People simply make way for us when they see you coming!"

"A man of many talents," he agreed equably. "Made your decision on the fish yet?" They were examining the offerings of a fishmonger who guaranteed to be able to pack the fish safely enough to allow it to last forty-eight hours.

"Let's risk that gorgeous salmon," she nodded and was glad that Simon handled the purchase. The fishmonger's rough and ready attitude toward his customers somewhat intimidated her. Simon had no problems. Five minutes later they were on their way, a huge package of ice-packed fish under Simon's left arm.

"The instant this thing begins to smell I'm going to chuck it, Kirsten," he warned, laughing down at her.

"Nonsense," she replied bracingly. "The man guaranteed it would travel, didn't he?"

"And just how do you propose to collect on the guarantee once we're back in Richland?" he inquired, lifting one brow.

"I'll leave that to you," she told him airily, consulting her map. "Now, we take a right here and walk three blocks down to the dock area."

She had to hand it to her escort. Simon carried the huge box full of salmon through an endless stream of import shops without a single grumble. Kirsten was beginning to worry about the weight of the thing when he called her attention to the new marine aquarium that had opened on one of the piers.

Moments later, seated in an arena surrounding a huge pool, she realized why he had been seized with a strong interest in watching killer whales leap for their food. With a sigh of relief the salmon box was lowered and Simon leaned back to enjoy the show.

"Onward and upward," Kirsten announced resolutely as they left the aquarium and started back toward the downtown area. "We'll catch a bus to Pioneer Square," she added sympathetically, eyeing the salmon box.

"You're too kind," Simon smiled with mock gratitude.

They toured the expensive little shops of the reconstructed historical section of Seattle, enjoying a glassblowing exhibition in the process and winding up in a pleasant bookshop. Kirsten was secretly pleased to discover Simon enjoyed browsing as much as she did.

"It's an occupational disease with a librarian," she explained.

"Book browsing? It's one of my favorite hobbies," he told her. She left him poring over volumes in the mystery section while she went in search of the science fiction.

Hours later they dragged themselves into the hotel, loaded with packages and shopping bags. Once in the room, Kirsten set down her burdens with a groan and kicked off her shoes.

"I feel like I've walked a marathon," she said, collapsing into a chair and studying her stockinged feet.

"I was the one carrying this damn salmon," Simon pointed out righteously, setting the box in a corner and coming over to sink into the chair opposite her.

"It will be worth it," she reassured him. "We'll have it baked with a good white burgundy . . ."

"Or a California Chardonnay? Yes, I think it will justify the effort. It's merely that, at the moment, I'm having a little trouble imagining the end product. That monster weighs fifteen pounds, you know!"

"A mere feather to you, surely?" she teased.

"Not nearly as delightful a feather as you," he told her, getting to his feet and lifting her upright with a gentle

125

hand around the back of her neck. His sensitive fingers played lightly with a few straggling wisps of hair that had loosened from the coil she had anchored earlier in the day with a clip.

"Do you lift all your women by the neck?" she inquired while his lips descended lazily to hers.

"Just you, kitten," he murmured and then kissed her. As before, the sensuous movement of his mouth on hers robbed Kirsten of anything but a desire to respond in kind. She wasn't even aware of her feet having left the floor until she felt the softness of the bedspread under her back. By then she was past caring. Her head was cradled against his left arm, the silver hook extending to one side. She felt Simon's hand at her throat in a gentle caressing movement and then it cupped her breast with a possessiveness that startled her at first. Then she relaxed, wanting the feel of his big, hard body against hers. Nothing else seemed at all important at the moment. She thrilled to the sound of his groan of desire, taking pleasure in the knowledge that she could arouse him as much as he did her.

Kirsten slipped one delicate hand inside his crisp white shirt even as she felt his fingers on the buttons of her blouse.

"Kirsten, honey, I want you so desperately," he muttered against her ear. "I need you, sweetheart!"

She didn't argue with him. Instead, she found herself pulling his tough strength even closer, telling him with her actions, if not with words, that she wanted him, also.

"You're mine, little one. I knew it from the first day!" The words were ground out in a low, intense whisper. "I swear I'm going to make you so aware of that fact, you'll be unable to even look at another man!"

Kirsten stirred beneath him, the import of his words sinking into her mind slowly. She wanted him, needed him, in a sense. But his possessiveness shook her. She remembered the way he had bundled Phil Hagood out the door much earlier in the day. Unbidden, the memory of his warnings against seeing Roger Townsend flooded her thoughts. She wanted Simon to want her but Kirsten knew

126

she could not suffer the humiliation of feeling owned again. She wanted a partnership, she reminded herself desperately, withdrawing in Simon's arms ever so slightly.

He was aware of her changed mood instantly.

"Kirsten? What's wrong, honey?" he muttered, concern masking some of the desire in the questioning eyes that met hers. "Don't be afraid of me, sweetheart," he whispered. "I'll take good care of you. You'll never have cause to fear me."

"Simon, please. I . . . I want to be sure . . ." Troubled gray eyes met his, pleading for understanding, and Simon's expression softened in response.

"I promise you won't have any doubts," he soothed, stroking a long fall of tousled hair back from her forehead. "Once you realize how much I need you and how you belong to me. . . ."

"Simon? Why do you keep talking about belonging? I know we want each other, but what about the partnership we talked about on the airplane?" Kirsten frowned, twisting slightly in his arms to meet his considering regard. "I can't let myself be completely dominated again, Simon," she ended pleadingly.

For a long moment the rugged lines of the face above her hardened and then a smile replaced some of the fading desire in Simon's hazel eyes. "Only you, my dear, would interrupt a passionate love scene like this with talk of a partnership! All right, much as it goes against the grain, I'll take a few minutes out to demolish your worries with facts. Number one, you never have been a dominated woman, so don't give me that line as a reason for being afraid! Dominated women don't leave their husbands after only two months of marriage! What I want from you is something Talbot never got!" He moved his very large hand gently over her mouth as Kirsten opened it to protest.

"Number two, the word 'partnership' was yours. I'm not certain what your definition of it is, but I can tell you now that I don't intend for us to live separate lives that only merge at certain points where we happen to share mutual interests. Or mutual desire." His deep voice took on the no-nonsense tones she knew so well. "I want to be—no—I *have* to be the most important thing in your world."

Kirsten stared at him, not having the courage in that moment to ask if she would be the most important thing in Simon Kendrick's world. Until she had that answer, though, she couldn't share his bed. A very female instinct sensed that the action would completely disarm her; put her in his power in a way she had never been in Jim Talbot's. She would truly be Simon's after that and there would be no chance to establish the sort of marriage she had determined she wanted. He would have her totally on his terms and he knew it. The risks of such a surrender were so great . . .

"Simon . . . I need time," she begged hesitantly, knowing that if he didn't choose to grant it, there was nothing she could do.

"We're going to be married next weekend, Kirsten," he growled, tightening his hold. "I won't wait much longer for you." A brief, reckless, wolfish smile touched his hard mouth. "And you'd hate me if I did!"

CHAPTER EIGHT

Simon seemed content to let Kirsten try and come to terms with herself on the matter of the marriage. As long as she settled things in her own mind by Saturday! At that point, he made it clear, he would be taking matters into his own hands, anyway. Such patience! she thought mockingly as she dressed for dinner that evening. But she couldn't bring herself to totally rebel and call off the swiftly approaching wedding. While one part of her pressed for a mutually acknowledged set of ground rules between them, another, more treacherous part wanted Simon on any terms—even his own.

The man was so much in her mind as she bent over the marble sink in the luxurious bathroom that she jumped a goodly distance when his knock came on the door. Hotel rooms lacked a certain degree of privacy.

"Damn!" Kirsten swore softly, dropping to her knees to hunt for the contact lens that had been jarred from the tip of her finger.

"Aren't you ready yet, honey?" Simon called.

"I was almost ready. Now it could be another half hour!" she answered somewhat caustically, groping through the pile of the rug while trying not to wrinkle her skirt.

"What's wrong?"

"I dropped my contact!"

"Let me in and I'll help you look for it. We've got reservations for seven and I don't want to be late."

Getting to her feet, Kirsten flung open the door. "It's all your fault, you know," she pointed out conversationally, facing him in her bare feet. Without her shoes the difference in their height took on mammoth proportions in her eyes. "If you hadn't pounded on that door when you did . . ."

Simon grinned down at her. "You've got that funny owl look on your face," he noted, bending over to drop a kiss on her frowning forehead.

"Honestly," Kirsten grumbled, "it's hopeless trying to nag you. You never take it seriously!"

"How seriously would you take being nagged by a little thing you can lift with one hand?" he asked reasonably. "Now stand back and let me see what can be done about this contact. I think we'll get you fitted with glasses as soon as possible. I don't intend to spend half our married life hunting for stray lenses!"

There was nothing to do but to stand out of the way. Kirsten watched him lift the white throw rug and flip it expertly. There was a tiny click and she saw the lens bounce onto the tiles. Snatching it up before it was lost again, she moved back to the sink, using the excuse of inserting the lens to avoid responding to Simon's last remark. The truth was, it had left her speechless. All she could remember was how Jim Talbot had always insisted she wear contacts because he said she looked so much more sophisticated without glasses. Simon didn't seem to care in the least. The thought warmed her.

They reached the restaurant that was perched high atop a sleek new bank building, and Kirsten was very glad she'd had something long and gracious to wear. Her hair was coiled at the nape of her slender neck, marking to advantage the low cut of the gown in back. The dress wasn't nearly as vampish as her red one had been, but it made her feel quite elegant and Simon seemed to approve. For some unexpected reason, Kirsten found herself lowering her eyes shyly from the look in his as he seated himself next to her in the velvet booth.

130

"You don't look so much like a kitten or a little owl tonight as a bright yellow butterfly perched beside me. Something tells me I won't ever forget your favorite color!" Simon whispered after accepting the wine list from the captain.

"You noticed!" Kirsten chuckled, glancing down at the soft yellow skirt of her gown.

"That first night I walked into your apartment it reminded me of falling into a swimming pool full of daffodils! It suits you, though. We'll have to put in some yellow rosebushes and maybe a bunch of yellow buttercups around the house," he added reflectively.

Kirsten looked at him, wanting to ask about the old stone house but not quite daring to bring up the subject of their marriage again. Instead she commented on the spectacular view of the city, and the conversation flowed along easy lines throughout the leisurely dinner.

The view was beginning to take on a fairy-tale aspect by the time they adjourned to the adjacent lounge. Kirsten suspected she'd probably had more of the good wine Simon had chosen than was wise. At a small window-side table Simon ordered after-dinner drinks, declaring her taste in them appalling.

"How could you have developed such nice taste in wine and still prefer something that resembles cough syrup after dinner?" he demanded teasingly.

"Not everyone can swallow molten fire," she grumbled, accepting the deceptive innocent-looking liquid he had requested on her behalf.

"Take a very tiny sip and sample it the way you would a new wine," he instructed, watching to see that she did as she was told.

Kirsten sipped cautiously. She didn't gag, but knew it was going to be some time before she took another swallow.

"You aren't by any chance trying to get me drunk, Simon, are you?" she asked carefully, eyeing him suspiciously across the rim of her balloon-shaped glass.

"You're already halfway there, sweetheart. I'm merely providing a push in the direction you're already heading," he told her smugly. "Let's dance. Don't worry," he added as she frowned doubtfully. "I'll support you."

Once on the floor he was as good as his word and Kirsten nestled happily against him, letting him steer her around. Blissfully she let her mind wander back to the days when she had thought him much too large for comfort. Now he seemed absolutely right.

"What are you giggling about, honey?" he inquired softly in her ear, pulling her tighter against him.

"How comfortable you are," she replied honestly, thinking she really was going to have to watch what she drank around Simon. When she was a trifle more sober all this giggling was going to be embarrassing!

"Comfortable, am I? Then perhaps the time is right to head back to the hotel," he said a little thickly.

Kirsten didn't offer a protest as he bundled her into the rental car some minutes later and wove his way through late evening traffic. She leaned back and admired big city lights until they arrived at the hotel. Without a word she allowed herself to be swept into the elevator, trying to look as dignified as possible in front of their fellow travelers. She was not certain she succeeded, however, judging by the smiles on their faces as Simon held her close to his side. She was satisfied to enjoy the feel of his arm around her, however, and decided not to worry about looking like his pet owl. Or was it kitten? Butterfly? Simon was going to have his own personal zoo if he married her, she thought happily. If?

"Get ready for bed, honey," he told her as they entered the room. To emphasize his words she received a gentle push in the direction of the bath. It was easier to keep going in that direction than it was to turn aside, Kirsten discovered, so she went ahead and did as she was ordered. The bed routine went by in a fog but a short while later she was in her nightgown, the pretty one with the ribbons and lace bordering the long skirt. After that it was almost easy to find her bedroom. She felt quite proud of herself. Rather vaguely she remembered Simon announcing that he would use the bed in what constituted the living room of the suite. Kirsten had just turned back the covers in a methodical fashion and climbed into bed when her door opened and Simon entered.

The first thing that struck her was that he wasn't wearing the silver hook. The white shirt he had worn to dinner was hanging, unbuttoned, around him and the left sleeve was empty. Poor Simon! Had he put his shirt back on after removing the prosthesis harness because he wasn't certain how she'd handle the sight of the stump? Kirsten decided to show him how little that mattered and opened her arms to receive him.

He came forward willingly enough, sinking heavily onto her bed and reaching down to scoop her against him.

"Kirsten, my little love." She heard his deep whisper and snuggled closer, the greater than normal intake of alcohol earlier in the evening taking its toll by making her sleepy. Simon's broad chest seemed an ideal location against which to pillow her head. The long soft hair, loosened from its confinement at the nape of her neck, floated gently around her shoulders and she was dimly aware of Simon running his fingers through it.

"Do you have any idea how much I want you?" he breathed against her hair before he stopped speaking and kissed her. It began as a slow, languorous caress that further relaxed Kirsten until she felt herself slipping backward to lie flat on the bed. Simon never let go, following her gentle descent with the full weight of his powerful body. Kirsten was distantly aware of the way her legs seemed suddenly trapped under his but couldn't manage to become in the least alarmed about it. Instead, as his tongue invaded her mouth, she worked one hand inside the loose white shirt and toyed happily with the curling hairs on his muscular chest, an act that seemed to arouse him even more.

Gentle kisses touched her everywhere—her mouth, her dream-filled eyes—and then began to travel down her throat to the point where the curve of her breast disappeared into the nightgown. A strong right hand took over at that point to push the material aside with a slow, steady movement that exposed her softness to his mouth in a tantalizing, inevitable manner. When Simon's tongue curled

133

tightly around one nipple Kirsten gave a cry of delight and locked her arms fiercely around him, urging him closer. His weight covered her completely, imprisoning her slender form beneath him until he shifted slightly to enable his right hand to continue its work.

Kirsten shivered in expectation as the nightgown was lowered to her waist.

"That's right, little kitten," he breathed in a deeply aroused murmur. "Come and curl yourself around me. I'll take care of you. You'll be safe and warm here in my arms."

The words acted as another caress, making Kirsten want to do exactly as he said.

"Simon, Simon," she moaned, reaching out to twine her fingers in his hair.

"What is it, sweetheart? Tell me what you want tonight!" he ordered against the soft skin of her stomach. The fingers of his right hand began to make seductive little forays beneath the lowered nightgown until Kirsten started to arch her hips with an unconscious, pleading need. She wanted him to touch her there. . . .

"Simon," she gasped. "I don't think I want you to leave me tonight," she got out in a tone of wonder.

"This evening when I held you close to me on the dance floor, I decided that I couldn't deny myself the pleasure of your bed any longer. But now I find I am a very greedy man, Kirsten," he whispered roughly. "I want so much more than your small, soft body, my love. I want all of you! Without any reservations on your part. Can you give me that or must I take it?"

She lifted longing eyes to the hazel depths above her, willing an explanation from him.

"Simon? Don't you want to stay with me?"

"With all my heart," he said with such passion, she knew he spoke the truth.

"Then why. . . ?"

His eyes glittered between narrowed lids in a look she recognized even through the sensuous fog in her brain. Suddenly she understood.

"You still want surrender, don't you?" Kirsten asked in

a small voice of dawning comprehension. She had thought Simon wanted her physical surrender and she had known that would be dangerous enough. But now it was unmistakably plain he wanted more. So much more.

"Complete and unequivocal." The terms were stated in a totally uncompromising tone, Simon's eyes holding hers in unbreakable bonds. "I want the kind of surrender you've never been able to give any other man—especially Talbot. Do you know what I'm talking about, Kirsten? I want to know you're mine, so completely mine, that you'd never think of leaving me under any circumstances. I could force the words from you, sweetheart. It's what I planned to do all evening. But now I realize that I want you to give them to me, little one. You can do it. Tell me of the surrender waiting there in your heart."

She shook her head, confused. "You're so certain . . ."

"You would have been so by now yourself if it weren't for the fact that you're still fighting the hatred Talbot instilled in you," he told her.

"But I don't hate him. At least, not anymore," she protested, and then listened to her own words with astonishment. It was true. Simon had driven the memory of Jim Talbot farther and farther away until she no longer cared about him one way or the other. For the first time in months she began to feel free.

"I know the man means nothing to you. He's not even important enough to hate. But he left a legacy to you, honey. He left you hating the soft side of your nature. The part of you that wants to give everything you are into the safekeeping of a man who will know how to treat your love. I'm that man, Kirsten. Accept that with your heart and your mind and all the indecision will be over."

"But, Simon, what are the words you want to hear?" she quivered.

"I want to hear you say you love me and trust me so much, you'd never leave me. Regardless of the provocation." His voice was very firm and certain.

Kirsten opened her mouth to dutifully repeat the phrase and then shut it again. "What do you mean, 'regardless of the provocation'?" she heard herself ask instead in a careful tone.

Simon smiled wryly. "Sweetheart, what would you do if I ever lost my temper with you?"

"What do you mean? You've already been upset with me on a number of occasions. . . ." Kirsten reminded him.

"I have yet to really lose my temper, honey. And, knowing you, it's bound to happen, sooner or later. So what will you do when that occurs? Run off in the middle of the night and file for divorce?" Simon watched her closely, the line of his mouth hard now, a waiting look in the patient eyes.

"Are you saying you'd beat me, Simon?" Kirsten whispered, stunned by the image of this large man in an uncontrolled rage.

"I'm asking if you would trust me not to hurt you seriously, even if I were furious. I want to know you're so sure of your feelings for me that you wouldn't let my anger drive you away. That *nothing* would drive you from my side. I could force the realization on you, sweetheart. I could make love to you until you'd say anything I wanted to hear and you know it. But, like I said: I'm greedy. I want the words to come willingly and wholeheartedly from the bottom of your warm little heart."

"Do you know how much you're asking?" she asked in a tiny voice.

"I'm asking for all of you. I told you that earlier," he smiled, leaning down to brush her forehead in an almost chaste kiss.

"What do I get in return?" she ventured.

"Do I seem like the kind of man who would demand more than he was prepared to give?" Simon asked almost lightly but with a depth of feeling that made Kirsten tremble. To have all of Simon . . .

Kirsten sensed the unyielding demand for trust and desperately wanted to satisfy this man who was coming to mean so much to her. But the memory of Jim Talbot's violence intruded. It might be true that the man no longer mattered to her, but the exposure to sheer brutality

136

couldn't be shrugged off so easily. What would she do if faced with a similar situation? She would not allow a man to beat her into submission. But surely Simon, for all his giant size, would never do such a thing to her. Jim Talbot had never given any indication of the violent side of his nature before marrying her, either, she reminded herself. Could she bring herself to trust a man so completely that she wouldn't bolt at the first hint of real fury on his part? Feeling as if she were becoming mired down in a quicksand of shifting emotions, Kirsten gazed helplessly up at Simon.

"Poor Kirsten," he finally said, smiling and shaking his head in what she could have sworn was amusement. "Here I am asking for a major decision while you're under the influence!" He leaned forward, kissed her lightly, and got to his feet. "You have a few more days, sweetheart. By Saturday I'll expect you to have reasoned out the whole matter in your usual clever fashion! Good night, honey, sleep well." Then he was gone.

Kirsten awoke in a somewhat subdued mood the next morning. She chose to blame it on the wine but knew better. Simon's parting comments the previous evening had shaken her. The man she was trying to envision as a husband strolled into her bedroom with a cup of coffee at the precise moment she was recalling the way he had held her before leaving. She was remembering his weight across her thighs when the deep voice greeted her. Startled, she snapped open her eyes and then turned quite pink.

"Good morning, Simon," she stammered, accepting the coffee gratefully. Then, seeking a light comment, "Coffee in bed? I know you promised to provide it but I didn't think you meant to start immediately!" The flippancy helped a bit. Kirsten leaned against the pillows and took a sip, holding the sheet to her throat with the hand that clutched the saucer. She had really slept soundly, she reflected, realizing she hadn't even heard Room Service's knock.

"I never say anything I don't mean, honey." Simon eyed her precarious grip on sheet and saucer. "You're going to

137

have it all over the bed in a moment. Which will you choose to save at the last moment? Your modesty or the coffee?"

"It's much too early for you to be grinning like that," Kirsten told him severely, setting the cup and saucer down carefully on the nightstand.

"You have a way of making me smile," he said with disarming simplicity. "Actually, though, I didn't come in to merely gaze upon your early-morning charms, lovely though they may be!" This was said with such cheerful lasciviousness that Kirsten couldn't help grinning in response.

"I'm crushed!"

"You should be. Somewhere between me and a bed!"

"Simon!"

"As I was about to say before being rudely interrupted, I thought you'd like to know we've got reservations for brunch at the Space Needle in an hour."

Kirsten absorbed the vital picture he presented standing beside her bed, crisp shirt unbuttoned as yet, the silver hook back in place. The thick, red-brown hair was slightly tousled, adding to the overall rakishness of his appearance. A pirate, she told herself, who could easily take what he wanted but chose to ensure the completeness of the final surrender by making his captive acknowledge her bonds.

And how could she ultimately do otherwise? she asked herself with an acute attack of honesty. She looked at him in the bright morning light and knew she loved him. It was an incredible relief to admit it to herself. If she felt like this, could the trust he also demanded be far off? She must be very certain before making that commitment. With this man there would be no turning back at the last moment because of fear.

"I'll be ready in time," she told him and suffered the indignity of a friendly slap on the rear as she reached out to grasp a robe.

"One of these days, Simon Kendrick . . . !" she began wrathfully.

"Promises, promises!" he taunted and disappeared.

The morning was fresh and brilliantly clear. They

walked the short distance from the hotel to the monorail terminal and boarded the futuristic train that had been one of the major attractions of the World's Fair held in Seattle several years earlier. It continued in service, ferrying passengers from downtown to Seattle Center, a bustling tourist park filled with carnival rides, exhibition halls, and the towering Needle. A glass elevator carried them to the top, where they stepped into a revolving restaurant. The city passed gently around below as they lingered over a gourmet brunch.

The conversation didn't lag. It never seemed to do so between them. But they didn't talk about the one subject that, in Kirsten's mind, at least, was uppermost.

That evening, after an afternoon spent cruising between islands on ferries, Simon turned the car in at the rental counter and, with the salmon package tucked safely under his arm, guided Kirsten through the airport to the line of passengers waiting for the plane back to Richland.

"The returning escapees," grumbled a young man on her left as Kirsten flashed the boarding pass for the gate attendant.

"Richland isn't that bad," she laughed, catching Simon's smiling gaze.

"Not a bad town at all," Simon chimed in, turning a superior look on the shorter man. "One simply has to learn to develop lots of outside interests."

An hour later they landed, the tri-city area shining like a glittering oasis in the middle of the night-darkened desert. Kirsten was quite ready for her bed when Simon brought the Mercedes to a stop in the parking lot of the apartment complex. It was going to seem dull not having him sleeping in the next room, she thought as they climbed out of the car. Nevertheless, it would be good for her to have some time by herself to think, she decided. She was unprepared for Simon taking a firm grip on her arm and guiding her toward his door.

"But this is your apartment," she observed unnecessarily as he gently pushed her over the threshold. "I'd love to stay for a while, but I think we both need our rest. Work tomorrow," she reminded him brightly, wondering what he was planning and knowing she was going to have to talk fast if she wanted to preserve her privacy. She needed a little more time to herself.

"Remember yesterday morning I told you I'd be making the morning coffee from now on?" He set the luggage down and snapped on a light. Kirsten took a quick look around. It was the first time she had been in his apartment. Even with the temporary furniture the room carried the unmistakable stamp of the man. Neat, conservative, and solid-looking. It occurred to her that Simon might be better at housekeeping than she was. She couldn't deny that her own place could best be described as "lived in."

Kirsten prepared to launch into a healthy protest when Simon walked toward a small cupboard and opened the door. She watched, astonished, as he withdrew the shoebox that had contained her late husband's lighter and decoration.

"So!" The single word carried a wealth of meaning, but she couldn't fathom it. All she saw was Simon lifting the lid of the shoebox. Kirsten stepped closer and peered over his shoulder.

"It's empty!" she exclaimed, surprised. "What did you do with Jim's things?"

"Gave them to a friend," he said succinctly.

"Gave them . . . What on earth for? And if you gave them away, why did you expect to find something in the box?" Kirsten was totally confused now.

"I substituted another lighter and someone else's Purple Heart before we left Seattle." Simon carried the box over to the coffee table and picked up the phone.

"Whose Purple Heart?" she demanded, for some inane reason seizing on that particular aspect of the mystery first.

"Mine."

"Oh."

"I phoned a friend and had him dig it out and send it to me earlier this week."

"I see," she answered, not seeing at all, of course. She was fairly certain she knew now how Simon had lost his

140

left hand, however. "Would it be presumptuous of me to inquire into why you went to all that trouble?"

But Simon was busy dialing the telephone and didn't appear to be receptive to further inquiries at the moment. Disgusted, Kirsten plunked herself down in one of the huge chairs (Simon had ordered furniture to fit) and waited to see what she could glean from the phone call.

"Rich? This is Kendrick. Sorry to get you out of bed. Oh. Well, in that case I'm especially sorry." This second apology was accompanied by a quick glance at Kirsten to see if she had been able to overhear the unknown Rich's comment. "Listen, we just got back and the Heart and Zippo are both gone. Yes, I know. You'll get someone on it? Okay. I'm keeping an eye on Kirsten. Night and day." Another quick, very male glance was directed at her from across the room. She returned it with her most innocent expression. He replaced the phone.

"I think," Kirsten said quite firmly, "that I deserve an explanation."

"And I think," Simon replied, equally firmly, "that you'll get one. In time. At the moment the first priority is bed. You'll find I'm not nearly so ungenerous as to offer you only a couch. Now, do you want to get some things from your apartment or do you have enough to enable you to get off to work in the morning in those?" He indicated her traveling bag and purse.

"It's academic. I'm sleeping in my own bed, Simon."

His eyes gleamed at her, and she knew she'd made an error in handling Simon Kendrick. She obviously had a great deal to learn on the subject. Before she got more than two steps toward the door, he had crossed the room and scooped her up with his right hand. The next thing she knew she was over his shoulder, being carried into the bedroom.

"Simon, put me down this instant!" she yelled, pummeling his back ineffectually.

"Hush, dear. What will the neighbors think?"

"I don't give a damn what they think! Maybe one will come to my rescue," she threatened furiously, not lowering her voice one iota.

"I told you what I'd do if you went recalcitrant on me," Simon smiled mockingly, flopping her down on the huge bed.

Kirsten rolled toward the edge and bounced off, putting it between them. "Simon, if you don't tell me what's going on around here I swear I'll . . ."

"You'll what?" he inquired pleasantly, regarding her with his right hand on his hip.

"I . . . I won't marry you on Saturday!" She tried the only weapon in her arsenal and waited tensely to see what effect it would have.

"Don't make threats you can't follow through on, sweetheart," he advised, moving toward the bedroom closet.

She watched as he rummaged around the overhead shelf. Except the shelf wasn't exactly over Simon's head. "I think I've got an extra pillow somewhere . . . ah, here we go." He tossed it toward her and she instinctively reached out to catch it.

"Simon, why won't you tell me?" she begged, lowering her tone humbly. "If it's anything to do with Jim Talbot, it's more my business than anyone else's!" She clutched the pillow protectively in front of herself.

Simon's face softened and she knew she was close to victory. Maybe she'd found the secret of handling Simon after all! Somehow, that was almost more important to her than satisfying her curiosity.

"I know you ought to have a full explanation, but it's a long story, Kirsten," he said gently, coming close and wrapping his hand around her neck in his usual method of ensuring her attention. "I don't know all of it, myself. It will only upset you if I go through it tonight, honey." The thumb moved around to massage the corner of her mouth in a sensuous manner. But she was determined not to be sidetracked.

"It will upset me a great deal more if you don't give me some idea of what is happening," she told him.

"All right," he said at last. "I'd prefer you trusted me a little longer, though." He watched her hopefully but she wasn't to be swayed at this juncture.

142

"This isn't a question of trust," Kirsten asserted pointedly. "This is a matter of satisfying my curiosity before I go crazy!"

He sighed. "The long and the short of it is I think your husband was running something—guns, dope, you name it. And I think Phil Hagood was in on it with him."

Without a word Kirsten sank down onto the wide bed, thoroughly shocked. "I don't believe it," she whispered, staring at the baseboard along the wall.

"Kirsten, I told you it would be upsetting," Simon began painfully.

"No, no. It explains so much!" she said in awe. "The absences, the way he closed me out of everything. But I don't understand how or why . . ."

"The why is easy. It's a very lucrative profession. The how is a bit more complicated. I think he got started in 'Nam and he and Phil continued the partnership when they returned to the States."

"But I thought that sort of thing was totally in the hands of the big crime organizations. . . ." Kirsten said slowly, finally able to tear her gaze away from the fascination of the painted baseboard.

"There's always room for small operators as long as they don't get in the way of the big boys. Talbot and Hagood were probably smart enough to stay small. Rich thinks they were dealing with small, independent groups. They'd learned enough in Southeast Asia to continue the profession after they got back to the States."

"But how did you guess all this?" Kirsten demanded, confused. "You didn't know anything about Jim and all you ever saw of his were the decoration and that old lighter."

"Those meant nothing to me immediately. But the name Hagood in Talbot's letter rang a bell. After I'd had a chance to think about it for a while, I called Rich . . ."

"Who is this Rich, anyway?" she interrupted.

Simon came over and sat down beside her, putting a considerable sag into the rented bed. "Rich Montgomery is an old friend of mine. We were together in . . ."

"Let me guess," Kirsten smiled ruefully. "In Southeast Asia?"

Simon nodded, ignoring her tone. "After I caught it and was sent home, Rich stayed on and became involved in some dope investigations. Drugs were a big part of the scene over there, Kirsten. All the armed services had groups dedicated to controlling it. Hopeless task for the most part, but Rich did a good job. Afterward, he went with a government agency . . ."

"He's a federal narcotics agent now?"

Simon shook his head negatively. "No. Another branch. He had shown a talent for undercover work and . . ."

"A spy!" Kirsten exclaimed, delighted.

One red-brown brow lifted warningly. "Am I going to be allowed to finish this tale or not?"

"Go on! What did the name Hagood mean to you and Rich?"

"Being a Marine, Rich used to get particularly upset when his early dope investigations uncovered . . ."

"Brothers of the Corps?" Kirsten suggested dryly.

"If you want to give it a melodramatic sound, yes," said Simon. "We've kept in touch over the years and on several occasions Rich mentioned the names of some individuals he was certain were running the stuff. He thought I might hear something from time to time. I didn't recall him ever mentioning Talbot, but I was fairly certain I'd heard the name Hagood from him. That note of Talbot's telling you to give the lighter and Heart to Hagood so he'd have something to remember started me worrying. I phoned Rich, who verified the name as someone he'd been unable to pin down during the war. He'd lost track of Hagood, having bigger fish to fry, but when I called out of the blue and started asking questions he got interested in a hurry."

"Which one of you decided the shoebox things were important?" she asked curiously, trying to take it all in.

"It was Rich's idea to investigate the contents more thoroughly. He sent someone over to pick them up on Tuesday. I'm the one who thought it might be interesting to replace them with substitutes to see if anyone would take the bait," Simon said with all due modesty.

"Obviously a stroke of genius," she told him admiringly. "You must have thought the vandalism of my apartment was more than just the work of some hoodlums?"

"After recognizing Hagood's name, I thought it likely. But I also thought that, having searched and failed to find anything, they'd leave you alone for a time. It was a whim on my part to make the substitutions. I thought if anyone came nosing around asking questions I'd let him know I had the box. Sure enough, Hagood showed up yesterday. While you were in the bedroom I let him know I had a couple of items of his dead buddy's. I told him I intended to contact Washington for some names of next of kin of Talbot's since you weren't interested in keeping them. Not because I cared a damn about the man personally, of course, but because he had been a Marine."

"An attitude Hagood could understand?"

"Ummm. Having dropped the bait, I got us out of the area so Hagood would have his chance. And he must have taken it because the box was empty when we got home tonight, as you saw." Simon pulled her against his right side, holding her tightly. "Does it bother you terribly, knowing Talbot was into something like this?" he asked quietly, and for the first time Kirsten understood his reluctance to tell her the whole story. He had been trying to protect her.

"Talbot was, as you informed Phil, a bastard. I could care less about the honor of his memory. I only hope your friend Montgomery gets things cleaned up quickly so we don't have to worry about Hagood or some associate jumping out at us from the tumbleweeds!" she announced with much feeling.

"Rich is good. He'll take care of matters. I forgot to ask him whether or not the lab had uncovered anything in the lighter or on the Heart," Simon mused, regretfully.

"It sounded as if your friend may have had other things on his mind tonight," Kirsten put in matter-of-factly.

"Ummm. The same sorts of things I have on mine, perhaps," Simon suggested lazily, hauling her closer.

"Nothing doing, Simon Kendrick! You've said, yourself, you aren't going to sleep with me yet, so I'm going home to my own bed!" Kirsten informed him roundly and then, seeing the determined glint in the hazel eyes, added pleadingly, "Simon, I have to have some time by myself to think. Everything's gone by in a haze these past few days. Please, let me have some time to myself to . . . to try and understand what's happening between us." Misty gray eyes gazed up at him, eloquently pleading her cause.

"Honey, I don't like the idea of you being alone with Hagood on the loose."

"He wouldn't bother me now. He's more likely to come after you when he finds out the Zippo and the Heart aren't Jim's," Kirsten pointed out logically.

"Maybe. No, I don't like it. I want you where I can keep an eye on you. You're staying here." But he was weakening in response to her gentle plea and Kirsten sensed it.

"Simon, I'll be perfectly safe. You can check the apartment over before you leave me behind in it. I need the time, Simon. Don't you understand? You've asked a lot of me and you can be very overwhelming. . . ." She was careful to keep her tone humble and beseeching. Ranting would get her nowhere. But she did want to be alone for a while. There was so much she needed to consider that couldn't be properly thought out with his disturbing influence nearby.

"Honey . . ."

"Please, Simon? You want me to be able to give you an honest answer to the question you asked last night, don't you?" They both knew she referred to his demand for an unconditional surrender.

"And you need privacy to come to terms with yourself?" he asked searchingly.

"Yes." It was the simple truth and it showed.

"All right," he agreed reluctantly, and pulled her close. "It's against my better judgment," he added grimly, his fingers stroking the nape of her neck as Kirsten buried her face against his shirt. She deliberately kept her nose pressed against him for a moment. It was necessary in order to hide the involuntary smile which had come with her victory over him. Simon could be handled, it seemed.

146

"I just hope for your sake, young woman, that this nasty feeling I've got of having just been 'managed' is nothing more than a false suspicion!" he added warningly, tightening his grip for an instant before releasing her.

"No, Simon," she assured him, turning quickly to head toward the living room and her luggage. He had told her once she had a very transparent face. It would be better if he didn't get a good look just yet.

"Ummm." He didn't sound totally convinced.

CHAPTER NINE

Half an hour after Simon had completed his precautionary
check of her apartment and reluctantly taken his leave,
Kirsten, dressed in a yellow nightgown, lay amid her yellow sheets and gazed at the ceiling. She had been completely truthful with Simon earlier when she had stressed
the need for some time to herself. Now she had it and
couldn't decide what to do with it. Did she really need to
consider the matter of marriage to Simon? she asked herself. No. It was a settled issue as far as she could tell. If
Simon wanted her, she would marry him. She loved him.
And when a small voice protested that she had only
known him a little over a week, Kirsten reminded herself
that she had known Jim Talbot much longer and never
felt as close to him as she did to her very large fiancé.

Yes, the marriage was settled. But what about Simon's
strange terms, Kirsten thought, staring at the pattern of
shadows above her. Could she give him the degree of surrender he wanted? Would he marry her without it? She
rather thought he would. He had said nothing about post-
poning the marriage until she came to him on his terms.
Was that because he was so confident she would do so
before the weekend arrived?

What right, she thought, did he have to demand so
much from her? The answer to that came quickly. Simon
assumed the rights he wished. Kirsten tried turning the sit-

uation around in her mind and looking at it from his point of view. He wanted her; had said she would have all of him if she was willing to give all of herself to him in exchange. All of Simon Kendrick? What an overwhelming notion! It literally filled her brain, leaving little room for rational thought. She remembered the way he touched her, the possessiveness he made plain. He would make a most demanding husband. Was she capable of satisfying him? For the first time a new worry intruded. Sex with Jim Talbot had been a demoralizing experience. He simply hadn't cared very much about the woman he was with, and she felt that was true of others as well as herself. He was interested merely in satisfying his own needs. Kirsten hadn't felt unsatisfied with him because he had never raised the level of her desire to the point where she craved fulfillment. She was intelligent enough and romantic enough to know there could be more to the experience, but it wasn't until Simon had touched her that she had glimpsed the tremendous range of feeling waiting to be explored. Simon was the only man she had begged to hold her! Didn't that say something about the emotions he aroused in her? After all, it wasn't as if she responded easily to a man. What was it that made her reactions to Simon so powerful? Love? Or some instinctive knowledge that she really could trust him. Totally and completely. Was that what her body was trying to tell her? Sleep claimed her before the answer came.

Kirsten had no idea how much time had passed when she heard the soft creak of the floor beside her bed. The sound made her freeze. The floorboard only protested in that particular fashion when someone stepped on it. . . .

For an eternity, Kirsten lay in chilled terror, her back to the source of the soft, ominous sound. It had ceased and she began to pray she had imagined it, even while common sense informed her it had been very real. Desperately, she tried to recall everything she had ever read about dealing with an intruder. Somewhere she thought she had heard it was best to pretend sleep. Let the thief go about his business without feeling threatened. Immobility proved easy enough. Kirsten wasn't at all certain she could move if she had to! Go on! she screamed in her head. The only money I've got is in the purse on the couch in the living room. Take it! Get out! With all her might she willed whoever it was to retreat back down the hallway toward the living room.

But when the sound came again she knew it was useless. What now? Make a dash for the window? Anything seemed better than waiting for God-knew-what to happen next. She had to make a decision. Better to begin screaming and at least try for escape. If the intruder was intent only on robbery, he would have moved on by now. A mind-shaking picture of a rapist with a knife, standing beside the bed, working up his nerve, was the final, motivating force.

An instinctive knowledge that she would have to fight, and the will to at least be on her feet when the battle came, drove Kirsten into a sudden, frenzied rush from the bed. She had some dim idea of putting its width between herself and the attacker. She opened her mouth to scream, remembering with a feverish gratitude the poor sound insulation between apartments. She staggered to her feet, drawing in a lungful of air. She was aware of the awful rushing noises around her, of dark figures moving with frightening speed to cover the distance to her. Figures! There were two men in the room!

The scream never escaped her throat. Some sort of cloth was wedged into her mouth the moment she opened it as gloved hands grabbed hold of her madly struggling body. The window was so close! Kirsten thought in despair, bending her whole will toward escape. She kicked out with little regard to possible damage to her bare toes. There was some gratification in feeling her foot connect with some portion of one of the attackers' anatomy. The angry, muffled complaint it elicited told her she had done some damage and she tried again. This time their patience apparently gave out altogether. One stepped behind her, held her arms very tightly, and the other stepped forward and lifted a clenched fist. An instant before the blow landed Kirsten finally got a look at Phil Hagood's angry features.

150

Then everything went painfully dark until unconsciousness took over completely.

Simon was right, Kirsten told herself miserably when she began to edge back into awareness. As usual. She wondered if he would ever let her forget it. The rueful thought helped restore her painful perspective and she allowed her eyelashes to flutter open. Automatically she tried to raise one hand to an aching jaw and realized with a shock that she was bound. Unable to touch the injured area, Kirsten immediately focused her whole attention on it. Had they broken bones? Had she lost any teeth? For a frightening moment she worried about the extent of the damage and then relaxed as her tongue detected no blood inside her mouth. Hagood or his partner had thoughtfully removed the gag. It was probably the fact that the thick material had been stuffed between her teeth earlier that had saved them, she reflected, realizing she could move her jaw in a reasonably normal fashion. Funny, people got clipped in the way Hagood had struck her frequently in films and on television. Strange that the heroes never made a big deal out of it. You're overreacting, my girl, Kirsten scolded herself. Quit worrying about details and try to get a handle on the situation.

The most noticeable fact was that it was dark. Kirsten had no way of knowing how long people stayed unconscious after being struck as she had been, but her internal body clock seemed of the opinion that not a great deal of time had passed. Sometime between midnight and dawn. Useful fact number one. It could be hours before anyone, namely Simon, noticed she was gone, Kirsten thought grimly. Well, stop thinking about the ramifications of the facts, she instructed herself. Gather the information first. Wasn't that the proper way to approach a research project? And she was nothing if not a good librarian, she reminded herself.

So on to fact number two. She was bound, hand and foot. Her arms were wrenched rather painfully behind her, but she still had feeling in her fingers, which meant things could have been much worse. She was lying on her side on rough, textured carpeting. It felt like the stuff used in indoor-outdoor floor coverings, she decided. Kirsten was congratulating herself on her powers of deduction when the biggest fact of all finally registered. The floor was shifting gently beneath her! It took several seconds for the full meaning to get through her somewhat clouded senses but she finally acknowledged that she was lying in a boat. And since she couldn't see the night sky overhead, presumably a boat large enough to have a cabin. The Columbia River was the only body of water around wide enough to float something of this size, Kirsten thought. Hagood and company had hidden her somewhere on the river. And they had removed the gag, implying she wasn't lodged within screaming distance of other boats or a populated shore. That left, she thought, a lot of river.

The knowledge that she was on the water seemed to heighten the chill that had begun to annoy her. Very carefully, Kirsten shifted herself gently. If she was in the cabin, she might be near a bunk or locker that would contain blankets.

She had explored one wall, or was it called a hull? bulkhead? to no avail, having only uncovered some lockers, when a sudden rustle of footsteps sounded overhead. A moment later a hatch was thrown open and Kirsten was suddenly blinking in the harsh light of a flashlight.

"Well, well. Sleeping Beauty has awakened. And without even waiting for the kiss of the handsome prince," Phil Hagood observed from somewhere behind the glare of the light he was holding. When Kirsten averted her eyes from the strong light he swung its beam to follow, pinning her beneath it. "Don't worry, Princess, there may be time for us later, when this is all over."

Kirsten said nothing. There was no sense provoking him with defiance at this point. Give the situation time to develop, she told herself, knowing that what she really meant was, give Simon time to find out what had happened and come to her rescue!

"Kind of nippy out here on the water tonight," Hagood went on conversationally. "Be sure and holler if you get cold," he instructed with a chuckle. "That little thin night-gown you've got on won't be much protection."

The wave of anger that washed through Kirsten's system at the callousness of Hagood's remark did much to temporarily warm her. So much so that she decided not to beg for a blanket or anything else from the man. Contenting herself with a gray-eyed glare, she stared past the torch in the direction of his voice. She could see his shadowy form, hear his soft laugh as an instant later he slammed the hatch shut again and left her in darkness.

Darkness but not silence. Kirsten could hear the voice of the second man now as Hagood and his partner carried on a low conversation. She spent a few minutes trying to discern the words, got nowhere, and resumed her search for a blanket.

It was a painful progress, but Kirsten consoled herself with the thought that the effort at least kept her mind focused on immediate problems and not long-range ones, such as whether or not she would get out of this mess alive. That sort of thing didn't bear speculation. She had to put her faith in Simon as far as the future went and concentrate on the problem of keeping warm.

It seemed hours before Kirsten discovered the storage locker that contained the blanket she had been praying for. It had taken several minutes to open the little door and keep it open long enough to grope around inside, but she had been patient. It was the fourth locker she had opened from the awkward position and her reward made the task worthwhile. Inch by inch she managed to unfold the old wool fabric and then she began to concentrate on how best to get it around her shivering body. The easiest solution seemed to be to lie on top and, catching an edge of the blanket between her fingers, roll herself in it until she was comfortably cocooned.

Feeling as if she had just won a great victory, Kirsten settled down to wait.

She didn't have long. A few minutes later the hatch overhead was again flung back and the flashlight projected downward.

"Got clever, did you? Jim was right when he said you

153

might be a little too smart," Hagood remarked, taking in the blanket. "Always did think he could handle anything, though, even a too-bright wife. Well, you can come out for a bit, Princess. We've got a small task for you."

Hagood dropped easily over the edge of the opening and clattered down the small wooden steps leading into Kirsten's prison. She watched him warily, frightened more about the possibility of losing her newly won blanket than anything else at the moment. Which only went to show that short-range problems had a way of looming larger than did more serious long-range problems, she thought, as Hagood yanked the blanket away from her feet, pulled out a knife, and slashed through the knots holding her ankles together.

"On your feet, my dear. Your lover will be glad to hear your voice, I'm sure!"

"Simon?" Kirsten breathed, speaking for the first time and regretting it instantly as she sensed Phil Hagood's satisfaction.

"None other," he told her cheerfully. "Don't get too excited, though. All we want to do is reassure the poor fellow you're still alive and kicking. You're going to get to chat with him over a telephone. Which reminds me," he added, fishing into his pocket and pulling out a length of fabric, "we don't want you giving out too thorough a description of your quarters to Kendrick over the phone, now, do we?" He proceeded to tie the blindfold around Kirsten's head, giving a small, sensual tug on the long hair as he finished. The small action made her shiver with disgust and she knew he was aware of it.

"It wouldn't be so bad, Princess," he murmured as he pushed her toward the ladderlike steps. "At least I have both hands!"

"You'd better keep both of them off of me or Simon will kill you," she shot back, goaded once again out of her silence.

"He'll never have the chance. Even if he did, he's been out of action a long time. Sitting behind a desk for a living doesn't do much for a man's muscle tone, you know. Now me, I've kept in shape." She could almost feel the man's mocking glance as she scrambled blindly up the steps. The only thing that kept her from falling backward was Hagood's hand in the small of her back. She wondered desperately how she could manage the final step out onto the deck of the boat when the question was abruptly answered. Another pair of hands reached down from above. She felt them close roughly under her arms and she was hauled out unceremoniously.

Steadying herself against the sway of the boat, Kirsten listened to Hagood and the other man discuss the next move.

"You'll do as I say and stay with the boat. I'll be back in half an hour," Phil instructed, obviously the senior partner in the venture. "I'll give Kendrick the orders, let him satisfy himself that his ladylove is all right, and then I'll be back. Satisfied?"

"Look, I just don't want to get left holding the bag on this thing, understand?" Kirsten listened to the other voice curiously. But other than the fact that it was male, sounded a bit desperate and nervous, she could tell nothing.

"Have I ever left you when your back was against the wall? Who was it who went back into the bush and dragged you out from under the noses of those guerrillas? Now will you just relax, for God's sake, and let me handle things?"

"All right, Phil," the other sighed unhappily. "Just don't be long, okay?"

"No longer than I have to. Come on, Princess, watch your step." Hagood grabbed her arm and moved her roughly to a gangplank. For the first time, Kirsten realized she still wasn't completely outdoors yet. Her bare feet moved cautiously onto a bobbing dock, feeling the wooden slats, and then Hagood reached around her and opened a door. A metal door, she thought. The boat was a shelter of some kind. There were no sounds outside to indicate that it was part of one of the large marinas along the river, which meant it must be a private boathouse. Which, in turn, meant it could be almost anywhere along the river.

Hobbling painfully over the rocky ground, Kirsten was forced along a drive and then into the front seat of a car.

155

Hagood climbed in beside her, started the engine, and maneuvered the car onto the smoothness of a paved road. Without a word, he drove for what seemed several miles and then brought the car to a halt.

"Listen close, Princess, because I'm only going to say it once. After I talk to Kendrick I'll put you on for a couple of minutes. Just long enough to let him know you're okay. Don't try to get anything more across to him than an indication of your undying love and the idea that your health is entirely in his hands. Clear?"

Without a word, Kirsten nodded her understanding. A moment later, she was pulled from the car, walked a few feet, and realized she was in the small shelter of a phone booth. With one hand holding her arm, Hagood dialed a number and waited.

The wait for Simon to answer his phone seemed as long to Kirsten as it must have to her captor. When it did happen, all she could hear was a faint click. Even standing as close as she was, Kirsten was unable to make out Simon's greeting.

"Kendrick?" Hagood began aggressively. "Don't say anything, just shut up and listen. You've got something I want and I've got the girl." Although he had just ordered Simon not to say anything, Hagood obviously expected some response to his remark, as did Kirsten. Both were disappointed. As far as Kirsten could tell, Simon didn't say a word. Hagood went on, a harder note creeping into his voice. "You know what I'm talking about, Kendrick?" Kirsten felt his grip tighten as he communicated his tension to her. "No, God damn it! I don't want the Heart! I want the lighter. The right lighter! It's got Talbot's initials on the bottom. You switched it, didn't you, you bastard? Well, I want it. Tonight! Tonight, or the woman is not going to see another night in your bed. Understand? Good. Here's what you're to do. Bring that Zippo to the entrance of Gravin Road. You know where I mean? Well, you damn well better find it then, hadn't you? I'll be there."

Hagood apparently thought it better to give directions than risk Simon asking for them at the local police station, because he then proceeded to give a brief description of how to find Gravin Road. The description gave Kirsten some idea of where she had been kept. It was a point along the river, several miles from town.

"Yes, you can talk to her. But only for a moment, Kendrick. I don't want to waste any more time!"

Abruptly the receiver was held against Kirsten's ear.

"Simon?" she said softly, not certain what to say, longing to hear the reassuring sound of his voice.

"Are you all right?" Simon's voice came low, hard, and sounded amazingly in command. It did not invite petty complaints, however, Kirsten decided with a glimmer of an inner smile, so she decided not to mention the clip on the jaw Hagood had given her.

"Yes," she replied simply, striving to sound equally crisp and calm.

"Is Hagood alone and how is he holding you? Be careful what you say," he instructed. "Try not to tip him off."

"Simon," she said quietly, "you won't forget to feed my two guppies, will you? And make sure the aerator is still working. It was giving me trouble earlier this evening." The aerator was housed in the little shipwrecked boat at the bottom of the tank. Would Simon get the picture? Beside her she heard Hagood's exclamation of disgust at the trite, womanlike remark, but he didn't yank back the phone.

"Don't worry, honey, the fish will be taken care of. I'm going to fry those two guppies for breakfast. Trust me?"

"Completely," she responded without even thinking, realizing as soon as the words were out that it was the truth.

"Ummm. Remember that when I'm giving you hell later on for having let you talk me into sending you back to your own apartment!" he advised. "Put Hagood back on the line."

But the other man was already grabbing the phone out of Kirsten's hand.

"You've got an hour, Kendrick. No more. Take one minute longer and the lady has had it. What? You're not in any position to make threats, pal. Just do as you're told." The receiver was smashed into its cradle and Kirsten found herself tugged roughly back to the car.

"Could you please remove the blindfold now?" she requested, amazed at the calm in her voice. But, then, wasn't Simon on his way?

"It's been my experience that a little bindness can be extremely effective in controlling a prisoner. Just like a little cold. Tends to make folks more manageable."

The casual ruthlessness of the remark made Kirsten realize Phil Hagood had kept prisoners before. What had he done with them? That question really didn't need an answer, she decided grimly. She and Simon both knew who he was and could testify against him. Hagood would have no option but to dump them in the river when he had what he wanted. Simon would recognize the fact, of course, and act accordingly. He certainly wouldn't be bringing the Zippo. He no longer even had it. It, at least, was safely in Seattle.

The long drive back to the dock was over too soon as far as Kirsten was concerned. Hagood removed the blindfold before leaving her behind in the darkened cabin again, but he took her hard-won blanket with him.

The cold was the worst part, she decided as she sat shivering helplessly. Her legs, at least, remained free, although her hands were tied. Occasionally she attempted to walk around the cabin, but the adventures usually terminated in skinned knees. Curtains appeared to cover the small windows, but there was no point trying to work them open with her teeth when she would only be confronted with the greater darkness of the boathouse. Hagood and his partner had left the small building, probably on their way to meet Simon.

The minutes ticked by with excruciating slowness. It would have to end sometime. Simon would take care of things, she thought.

It was so quiet. Then it wasn't so quiet any longer. Over her head the hatch opened. She could hear it more than see it. The only thing her eyes could truthfully detect was a faint change in the quality of the darkness in that particular region. But it did change. And there was no sudden glare of a flashlight or the shouted instructions of her captors. Kirsten held her breath, knowing instinctively who had lifted the hatch.

"The Marines to the rescue?" she asked, feeling somewhat light-headed.

"I'm here, honey. Keep quiet," Simon ordered.

The relief was dazzling! Simon had pulled it off, just as she had known he would. There was a small scraping sound and then she could feel his presence filling up the tiny cabin. For all his size he made barely a sound.

"Over here," she breathed. "My arms are tied." She felt his hand grope and then make contact with her cold arm. The strong fingers slid down to the ropes that bound her wrist.

"Right. Hang on a second. I've got a knife." His tone was clipped and totally unemotional. How could he be so calm, she wondered dazedly. A moment later she felt the pressure as her bindings resisted and then gave way beneath the thrust of Simon's knife. With a small murmur of relief she sagged into his arm, delighting in the brief hug he allowed her.

"You're all wet!" she gasped, surprised.

"So will you be in a minute." She thought there was a smile in his voice now. "You're going to have to swim for it, sweetheart. You can swim, can't you?" he added as an afterthought, loosening her grip and guiding her toward the small steps to the hatch.

"Yes, but . . ." Kirsten's voice trailed off as she contemplated the coldness of the river water. She was feeling almost frozen already! Still, there was nothing she could say. If Simon had decided the most expedient way out of the situation was to swim to shore, then that probably was the best option. It was just bad luck that she was already so very cold.

"But what, Kirsten?" he prodded just before lifting the hatch.

"Nothing, Simon. I can swim as well as any fish!"

"Good. I thought you probably could. Now, follow me and try not to make the smallest sound, understand?"

"Yes."

Simon helped her protesting muscles make the climb out onto the deck of the boat. The door to the boathouse was still closed and Kirsten realized he must have swum underneath the wall in order to surface inside near the boat. A minute later, she understood that was how they were going to exit the scene also.

She watched as Simon slipped into the cold water and then reach up for her. His dark form was barely visible against the darkness.

"Sink in as quietly as you can," he ordered. For the first time she realized he was not wearing the hook. Probably didn't want to get the webbing wet, she thought, as she followed instructions and slipped over the edge of the boat.

It was cold. Every bit as cold as she had imagined it would be. Stifling a gasp, Kirsten shut her mouth firmly against any complaints and followed the guiding tug of Simon's hand. It must be awkward to swim with only one hand, she thought as he released her with a whispered order to follow him. At the boathouse wall he took a breath and ducked under the water. Kirsten followed suit, wondering if she would ever be warm again.

And then they were on the other side. It was still dark, but now she could make out Simon's half-nude form more clearly. They weren't far from the water's edge, although it seemed like the longest swim she had ever made. When her feet touched bottom she automatically attempted to stand, only to be pulled down smartly.

"Stay low, for God's sake. They aren't that far away!" Simon hissed.

Trembling, Kirsten crawled over the slippery, rounded river rocks on her hands and knees, the night air striking her cold skin brutally. They were protected by the incline of the land as it sloped to the river's edge. Low scrub trees and an assortment of weeds provided more cover as Simon led her in a crouch for several yards. When at last he straightened, she almost couldn't imitate the action because of the weakening effect of the damp cold. Simon pulled her close, listening for a moment like an animal trying to sense his surroundings, and then he bent low.

160

"The car is parked about a hundred yards farther along. Just follow the river and you can't miss it. The keys are under the seat. There's a blanket in the trunk. Get it and get into the car. Wait half an hour. If I'm not back, drive immediately back to town and get help. Do you understand?"

"Simon! Why aren't you coming with me?" she choked, shocked that he would risk everything now that they were free.

"I'm going to fry a couple of guppies for breakfast." He grinned and in the faint light she could see the flashing white of his teeth.

He's enjoying this, she thought furiously. He's looking forward to taking Hagood and his friend all by himself!

"Simon, that's stupid! Come back with me for the cops. Let them handle this!" she argued.

"Hush, honey, and do as you're told. And I mean exactly as you're told! If we drive all the way back for help, it's a cinch those two jokers will get away. I'm not letting that happen. Now move!

He slipped away into the darkness, not giving her a chance for further protest. In mute astonishment and anger Kirsten watched him as he was absorbed into his surroundings and then she turned and started off slowly in the direction of the car. She had taken about forty steps when she began to think better of the idea. True, she would be warmer in the car but the suspense of waiting for Simon's return would be almost unbearable. In a burst of decision, Kirsten came to the conclusion that she was not the type of woman who could sit meekly awaiting her warrior's return. She would follow him.

Once again trying to put the cold out of her mind, she slipped into the brush in the direction Simon had disappeared, grateful for the ballet instructions and the fencing lessons her father had insisted upon so many years ago. For the first time in her life she found a use for the delicate way one could move on feet that had been properly developed.

It wasn't until the quarry popped unexpectedly into view that Kirsten stopped congratulating herself on her

161

stealthy movements and was brought forcibly back to reality. The sight of the two figures sitting in the parked car caused her to retreat instantly back over the small rise she had just topped. Heart pounding, she collapsed onto the ground, abruptly terrified that just because she had spotted them, Hagood and his pal would know instinctively she was in the vicinity.

Be realistic, she told herself severely. They don't suspect a thing yet. Stay calm and stay clear. Simon won't thank you for interfering at this point! In fact, what would Simon say when he found out she had disobeyed his instructions? No, orders. Well, she'd worry about that when the time came. Right now it seemed vastly more important to stay as close to him as possible.

The silence stretched on for a few more minutes. Kirsten wondered what the two in the car were thinking. Surely the hour they had allowed Simon would be just about up? And what was Simon doing, for that matter? How could he take the two men as long as they were safely locked in the car? Or were the car doors locked? So many unknowns!

The speculation came to an end with the angry slamming of a car door.

"He should have been here by now!" Hagood's voice snapped. "You stay with the car. I'm going to see if I can spot any car lights coming. He knows better than to bring along the cops, for God's sake!" The anger was overlayed with a touch of worry that was not lost on the other man. The second door slammed and Kirsten realized both men would be out in the open by now.

"Let's get out of here, Phil. I don't like this set-up. It feels wrong. You know that as well as I do. Let's get rid of the girl and get out!"

"You fool! We can't leave Kendrick behind. He knows me!"

"So? You can disappear. If we can get that electronics stuff out of the country so easily, we can get you out. Come on, Phil. Pack it in!" There was a pause and then the man burst out, "Please, Phil! Let's get out of here. Nothing's gone right since Talbot died!"

162

"Can't you understand, you fool? Nothing's going to go right until we have that list! We've got to get it or kiss the whole business good-bye!"

"Phil, listen to me . . . Phil!"

Kirsten caught the panic in the man's voice just as she was aware of a soft thud. The unmistakable sound of something the size of a man hitting the ground.

Then Simon's voice snarled into the night. It came from a point several yards to her right, uphill from the river.

"Don't move or you'll join him!"

In spite of herself, Kirsten went as motionless as the one to whom Simon had issued the order. She could tell, even though she couldn't see him, that Hagood's friend was terrified.

"You killed him!" the strange man finally whispered.

"He'll live," Simon announced laconically, his voice coming from a different point now, closer to the car. "Get over there beside him, put your hands on your head, and kick the gun in my direction. Move!" This last remark sounded very similar to the manner in which Simon had issued the same order to her several minutes earlier, Kirsten thought with a grimace, still keeping out of sight behind the brush-covered rise.

It was inconceivable to Kirsten that anyone could willfully disobey Simon when he sounded as coolly violent as he did now. Therefore it came as a shock when there was a sudden scramble and a shot rang out.

"No!" The word was torn from her throat as Kirsten clambered to the top of the small rise, absolutely certain she would find Simon's body on the ground. She couldn't bear it! He must be all right! Her conviction that he might be badly wounded was so great that she had trouble taking in the scene that met her as she finally got a view of the three-man play going on below her. Hagood's body lay unmoving on the ground. The other man had fired a shot with the gun he was supposed to be kicking and now he swung around in her direction, the weapon held in a panicky, unprofessional grip. It was probably the only factor that saved Kirsten's life. She didn't need Simon's thundering yell to get down to send her flat onto the ground. The hastily squeezed off second shot missed her by a couple of feet, but it felt a good deal closer.

There wasn't a third shot. A thud made Kirsten lift her head in time to see Simon send the full weight of his strong body against the gunman, knocking the gun from his grasp. She scrambled once again to her feet and then tore down the incline, intent on retrieving the gun from the fingers that had suddenly come to life near it. Phil Hagood was far from dead! Simon must have known that. It was the reason he had taken the risk of forcing the other attacker to kick the gun away. There was no doubt that Hagood wounded was still a more dangerous threat than his pal.

She wasn't going to make it! Simon was totally involved overcoming the frenzied struggles of his victim and that meant Kirsten was going to have to do something quickly. Bending low, she scooped up a handful of small rocks and sent them sailing with remarkable accuracy. They did no damage, but the sharp peppering caused Hagood to wince, duck his head, and momentarily forget about the gun. In the next instant, Kirsten had it safely clutched in her own hand. It was then she noticed the odd-shaped object with a cord near Hagood's head.

She withdrew a couple of feet to a point where she could keep an eye on Hagood and watch Simon and the other man at the same time. The battle on the ground was practically over already. Simon paused for a moment to make sure the other was truly subdued and then bounded to his feet, glittering gaze swinging instantly to take in the tableau of Kirsten standing guard over Phil Hagood.

"Where the hell did you learn to handle a gun like that?" were his first words as he assessed her stance with a knowledgeable eye. The soft light of a late-rising moon was now illuminating the scene and Kirsten caught the glint of the hook at his side. He must have replaced it after leaving her, she thought, and then answered his question.

"From a Marine." She could see one dark eyebrow lift

in further inquiry. "My father," she added by way of explanation.

He nodded briskly. "Then since you know what you're doing, you can watch them both while I get something to secure them with."

A few minutes later, Simon completed his task, hesitating over Hagood long enough to strip off the man's jacket. Rising, he moved over to Kirsten and pulled the garment close around her shoulders. Grateful for the warmth at last, Kirsten glanced at Hagood where he lay bound in more of the same rope he had previously used on her. The man did not look as if he were interested in her thanks for the coat, however, she thought with a small smile, and withheld her remark.

"I'll take that now," Simon commented, removing the weapon from her hand and spinning her around by the shoulders to face him. For the first time Kirsten realized he was angry. Blazingly so.

"If you think," he began in an unnaturally even tone, "that you can manage to follow orders this time, take my car and drive to the nearest phone. Call the police and then go straight on home. Is that understood? Get into a hot shower and have a cup of something warm. I'll be there as soon as I can. And I'd better find you waiting up for me when I get there! Don't imagine for one minute that you're going to get off lightly for the damn fool stunt you pulled here tonight!"

"Simon?" Kirsten asked hesitantly, a small shiver going through her that wasn't generated by the cold. He was furious!

"Don't say another word, Kirsten. Do as you're told. Here." He tossed her a bunch of keys taken from Hagood's car. "Drive their car back to where mine is parked. Your feet must be torn to ribbons by now. Move, woman!" he snapped as Kirsten still hesitated, clutching the coat at her throat.

She moved. It was as she drove past the grim little scene of Simon and his prisoners that she saw him scoop up the corded metallic object that she had noticed beside a stunned Hagood. A weapon of some sort? But where would Simon have gotten something odd like that? And then she forgot the problem as she settled down to the task of driving a car without her contact lenses.

CHAPTER TEN

The shower recommended, or rather ordered, by Simon did wonders for Kirsten's sense of physical well-being. She stood beneath the full blast of the hot water and let it work the lingering cold out of her bones. From now on, she promised herself, she would stick to heated pools when she wished to swim! Blissfully she pivoted beneath the spray and wondered if the police now had everything in hand. Simon should be home soon, she thought, and abruptly remembered again that terrible moment when she had heard the first shot fired by Hagood's partner; the one she thought had killed Simon. Never, ever did she want to live through that kind of fear again! Now she knew what real fear was, Kirsten reflected grimly. It was a crushing, hopeless feeling that you were powerless to help the one you loved. Her fears of Talbot's brutality and Simon's size didn't begin to measure up to the real thing, she decided.

Putting that recollection aside, Kirsten stepped, dripping, out of the shower stall and reached for a yellow towel. Strange, she reflected, how she had never doubted from the beginning that Simon would rescue her from the kidnappers. Viewed in the harsh light of reality, it had been an illogical assumption. The statistics on kidnap victims were hardly encouraging to read! But the conviction that Simon would come to her rescue had kept terror at bay during the long cold time on the boat. Her chief reaction to Hagood and his partner's threats were anger and irritation. The knowledge that Simon would take care of everything had crystallized even more firmly in her mind when he had asked her on the phone if she trusted him. Of course she did! How could she ever have doubted it?

"And why, my girl, were you so sure of Simon's ability to get you out of that particular mess?" she demanded of herself in front of the mirror. Because she belonged to Simon, her foggy image smiled back as if she was displaying an uncharacteristic lack of intelligence. It was as simple —and as profound—as that. Simon Kendrick would always take care of his own.

Now, when she examined her heart with honesty, she knew the knowledge that she could give herself completely into Simon's large hand had been slowly growing from the first. She could not imagine having allowed any other man to force his presence on her for an entire night as Simon had that evening when she had returned home to find the apartment ransacked. Kirsten shook her head ruefully as she slipped into a long-sleeved nightgown and matching robe. She should have asked herself a few pertinent questions then! It might have saved a deal of trouble.

Beginning to hum softly, Kirsten found her yellow fluffy scuffs under the bed and then walked down the hall to the living room. Simon's instructions had included having a hot drink. It was too late at night for coffee and she really felt the need for something more warming. She owed it to herself. There was nothing else in the apartment except a carton of milk and her collection of wine. What she really needed, Kirsten decided, was some of Simon's fiery brandy. Yes, that would be just the thing. Had her pirate left in such a hurry tonight that he might have forgotten to lock his door?

A few minutes later she was trotting briskly down the sidewalk in her robe and slippers to Simon's apartment. The door handle turned easily in her grasp and she let herself inside with a distinct feeling of pleasure. She would wait for Simon in his own apartment. The brandy was soon located along with a balloon glass and Kirsten curled up in a corner of the huge couch to drink it.

The effects of the potent drink were more soothing than reviving, however, and, setting the glass down carefully on an end table, Kirsten allowed her eyes to close for a few minutes. She had no idea how long the few minutes lasted because the next thing of which she was aware was the slamming of the front door.

Blinking sleepily and looking somewhat like a yellow kitten that has just been rudely awakened, she glanced up to find a very angry Simon standing with his back to the door, glaring at her from across the room. In the instant before he started toward her, Kirsten could have sworn there was another emotion underlying the fury. Fear? Why should he be afraid? she thought wonderingly.

Whatever had been reflected in the hazel gaze was fast disappearing as the dominant emotion of anger pushed out anything softer. Kirsten found herself unable to move as he strode purposefully across the room. One part of her still-sleepy mind absorbed the fact that he was wearing the work shirt and damp jeans. She wanted to tell him to follow his own instructions and take a hot shower, but the forbidding cast of his features did not invite such remarks.

"I thought," he began very carefully, coming to a halt directly in front of her, "that I told you to go home and wait for me. I assumed you would head for your own apartment! Do you have any idea what I went through just now when I couldn't find you there?"

Kirsten said nothing, wary of the smoldering look in the furious gaze that was pinning her to the couch. Mutely she shook her head very slightly, her hands beginning to clench together tightly in her lap. She wished she had the courage to untuck her legs, which she very much feared had gone to sleep in their curled position.

"When I didn't find you where I had expected to find you, it looked as if you might have been afraid to face me. As if you had flown the coop. All in all," he concluded with an unpleasant softness in his rough tone, "it proved to be the last straw in an otherwise disastrous evening." He watched her for a long moment, right hand braced on his hip.

Kirsten sat very still, afraid to provoke him further and

169

convinced that nothing was going to swerve him from his present course. She had better prepare herself for a nasty few minutes, she thought with resignation. Wide-eyed, she waited, gray gaze fixed on his thunderous face.

"I think," Simon went on righteously, "that I have been extremely patient with you." Kirsten kept her own counsel on that subject. "I also think that the time has come to take steps to preserve my future peace of mind. I want you to understand, sweetheart, that what I am about to do is not simply for your own good, nor is it merely a means of letting you know who will be the ranking *partner* in our marriage. With any luck, it will serve those purposes. But that's not nearly as important as the immense personal satisfaction I will take from it!"

"Simon!" Kirsten got out at last, reading his intention now. "What are you going to do?" Stupid question.

"I am going to whale the living daylights out of you!" With that his right hand moved, lifting her off the couch before she could dodge. Just as quickly he had switched places with her and then she was across his knee, gazing at the pattern of the rug. But before she could come to any aesthetic appreciation of the gold and brown design, Simon's hand was being applied to her backside in a series of sharp, heartfelt slaps.

Kirsten caught her breath and yelped with pain and surprise. She struggled, but to no avail as his left arm firmly anchored her in position.

The whole thing was as embarrassing as it was painful and it was only the thought of the close proximity of neighbors that kept Kirsten from yelling blue murder. When the punishment ceased at last she was allowed to slide to a kneeling position between his knees. Simon still held her firmly with his right hand around the nape of her neck. He regarded her shocked, pained gaze without any sympathy whatsoever, totally ignoring the dampness of tears that threatened briefly. Kirsten hastily got them under control, knowing they were caused as much by her own emotions as by the spanking. And the emotions were those of joy generated by this new confirmation of Simon's char-

170

acter. Even in a fury, he had never lost his self-control. Just as, deep down, she had known he would not.

"Another thing, my future wife, don't think for one minute that I'll ever again let you trade on the fact that I love you to distraction! I was a fool to let you go back to your apartment alone tonight! I knew I should have kept you in my bed where you belong! Nothing would have happened if I hadn't given in to your pleading! My God! What I went through until I had you out of that boat! Then you had to go and disobey me! Disrupt a situation which I had completely in hand!" With an exclamation of profound annoyance, Simon let go of Kirsten's neck and reached for the half-full brandy snifter. He downed the remaining contents in one satisfied swallow and returned to his lecture, apparently renewed. He opened his mouth to further admonish his victim and abruptly shut it again, a look of surprise and dawning wonder replacing the outrage in his eyes. Kirsten continued to regard him warily from her position on the floor. There was a long silence while he stared at her and then Simon spoke very softly.

"I don't suppose it has yet occurred to you that I just finished administering a rather sound beating?" he said a little thickly.

"I don't see how I could fail to be aware of it," Kirsten replied with great feeling, one hand going automatically to the portion of her anatomy that had suffered most severely.

"You don't look," he observed slowly, "as if you intend to run away at the first opportunity." His hand reached out to touch the tendrils of hair that had loosened from the knot at the back of her head.

"Now, why would I do that when I love you more than anything else in this world?" she inquired, knowing her damp eyes must be reflecting the warmth and love she was experiencing for him. "Could you go over the part about loving me to distraction, please? I want to make sure I got everything I should out of the lecture. A woman who loves and trusts a man completely, as I do you, doesn't like to miss a thing he has to say!"

"Kirsten! Are you quite, quite certain? You're sure now

about your feelings?" Simon's rich voice was laced with a kind of desperate concern.

She grinned mischievously. "I told you earlier this evening all I needed was some time alone to work out my answer!"

The pirate grin suddenly appeared as Simon reached down to pull her onto his lap. "I imagine I shall have to be grateful for the results and just ignore the fact that the time you took must have aged me by about ten years! I knew I would lose my temper with you someday, but I had hoped it would be long after I knew for certain you wouldn't leave me when it happened. But when I walked in tonight to see you sitting there on my couch all soft and yellow and looking for all the world as if nothing out of the ordinary had happened, I couldn't help myself. I don't think I've ever been so angry with anyone in my life as I was with you when you came racing over that hill, straight into Jensen's line of fire! Here I had been thinking you were safely out of the action, on your way home! I was terrified you would get hurt and I promised myself that if we got out of the situation alive, I would first pound your rear until you'd think twice about disobeying orders in the future and then make love to you until you begged for mercy! I managed to cool down somewhat while waiting for the police, but when one of them finally dropped me off and I went straight to your apartment only to find you gone, I came unglued all over again! Kirsten, why didn't you do as I told you after we climbed out of that damned river?"

"I couldn't bring myself to drive off not knowing what would happen to you. When I heard that shot I was certain that man had killed you! For a moment then nothing else in the world mattered!" Kirsten lifted a finger to trace the hard line of his jaw. "If you were dead, I didn't care much about living, myself."

"Sweetheart, I love you very, very much. Do you know that?" Simon smiled gently, holding her close against his warm chest. Kirsten slipped her hands under the loosely hanging shirt and sighed happily.

"Simon, do you think I saw you at your angriest tonight?" she asked curiously, concentrating on the button that was in her line of sight as she lay cradled against him.

"Believe me, honey, nothing you could do would infuriate me more than what happened tonight!" he confirmed positively.

"Not even if I were to make eyes at another man?" she pressed impishly.

"That's an issue, thank God, which will never arise," he stated with absolute certainty.

"How do you know that?"

"Because you're mine. I think you've realized that at last, haven't you, little one?" The demand in his words made Kirsten lift her eyes. The look of love and fierce possession in his hazel gaze that met her gray one made her catch her breath.

"Oh, yes, Simon. I know it. I should have known it much earlier!"

"I thought so. Now, why are you trying to find out if I could ever get any more furious than I was tonight?" he queried, refusing to release her gaze.

"Because . . ." She hesitated, searching for the right way to express her feelings, her knowledge. "Because even when you turned me over your knee, you never really seemed out of control. I know you thought you were at the end of your patience, but I also know you would never have seriously hurt me. Do you understand what I'm trying to say?" She looked at him worriedly. How could she explain that she had known the difference at last between a man who could not handle his own anger and one who could express it forcefully without losing his own self-mastery? Between a man who could desire her and one who could combine that desire with love?

"Kirsten, I could never bring myself to damage, either mentally or physically, my own brave little falcon," he whispered huskily. "But that does not mean I don't intend to keep her chained very closely to my wrist in the future!"

"Am I a falcon now? I'm going to have an identity crisis if this keeps up! I've been a kitten, a butterfly, an owl . . ."

"Isn't it fortunate that I have a fondness for small creatures?" he asked softly, lowering his mouth to hers in a kiss that seemed to convey the full spectrum of his character. In it Kirsten experienced strength tempered with a gentleness she knew she could trust, a man-sized hunger that she wanted only to assuage and then rekindle, and an unrelenting possessiveness that both thrilled and weakened her in a way she had never known before.

• "I think," he announced with a sort of grim determination a moment later, "that I'm going to move up the wedding date!"

"Simon," Kirsten said very seriously, brows coming together in the look that he identified as owlish but which she chose to consider serious, "you must know you don't have to marry me. I mean . . ." Her voice trailed off rather helplessly and one graceful hand moved slightly to indicate the complete willingness with which she nestled in his arms.

"Don't I?" He grinned wolfishly. "I've got news for you, little one. I won't be able to sleep at night until I know I have you bound to me by all the laws of God and man! I'm much too old to spend my days running after an independent woman who can't be bothered with wedding vows! I find I need the reassurance of my ring on your finger and the knowledge that the world will know you as Mrs. Simon Kendrick. I don't want anyone else to have doubts about who owns you!" He nodded his head wisely. "I think we'll be married in the morning!"

"I won't have time to get tuxedos for my fish!" Kirsten giggled and then smiled. "Besides, I don't see how you could possibly schedule it that quickly. There are such details as blood tests and waiting periods!"

"And there are little things like being within a three-hour drive to the Idaho border where a little town called Coeur d'Alene specializes in reducing the total waiting period to about one hour. Including blood tests!"

"Simon! How do you know about that?" Kirsten stared at him.

"That Coeur d'Alene is to Washington what Reno is to California? I made it my business to find out the most ex-

174

pedient method of getting married shortly after I met you, my love! I knew the day you walked into my office and let me know I could go to hell with your job that I wanted all that fire for myself! I also knew you didn't find the corporate world any more satisfactory than I did. Why do you think I teased you by pointing out the similarities to the military structure?"

"Simon!"

"Then I read your businesslike report justifying a research library for a company that isn't even in a position to provide free coffee to its employees and realized your talents were being wasted. You'll be much better at marketing wine, honey! You're so small and so strong, my little Kirsten, I could hardly believe it! I knew you were fully capable of going through life alone and the knowledge hurt. I wanted to convince you that you needed me. That you could trust me. I was prepared to give you a little time, but when you showed signs of being even slightly interested in someone else besides me, I knew I couldn't wait."

"I am obviously marrying a man of single-minded determination," she marveled.

"I'm pleased you realize it. And since I'm tired of lounging around in damp jeans, I suggest we repair to the bedroom, where I can slip into something comfortable." He grinned with satisfaction.

"A warm robe?" she suggested politely.

"I had in mind a warm bed," he returned casually. "Now, why are you suddenly turning all tense on me?" he asked, setting her gently on her feet and rising to tower over her. "Didn't you know, sweetheart, that I could never let you go to bed without me again?" His eyes darkened with a possessive passion. "If you're thinking that you can put off the moment of belonging to me until you've had another chance to think things through, I've news for you . . ."

"No, Simon," Kirsten interrupted quickly, her hands moving up to settle on his shoulders, her expression earnest. "I've accepted the fact that I belong to you in a way I've never understood before," she said simply and with such a touching sincerity that he instantly pulled her closer. But Kirsten wedged her hands between them. "That's not an issue in my mind any longer," she continued.

"Then why are you suddenly so nervous, honey?" he pressed determinedly.

"You seem to have known all along that you could make me yours." Kirsten touched a tongue to her lip. "But I . . . I've never had quite the same feeling about you. Oh, Simon, I couldn't bear it if you didn't need me as much as I need you! I want to know you're mine as much as you know I'm yours!" she finished in a panicked little rush of words. Whirling chaotically in her memory were images of the way she had come to her first marriage, prepared to give and receive affection. But Jim Talbot had been incapable of either and had thrown it all back in her face. Now she was committing herself to an infinitely greater extent to a man who demanded far more of her than Jim had even realized existed. One could forget a man like Talbot; walk away and build a new life. But there would be no easy way to leave Simon behind. She knew it as surely as she knew the sun would rise.

"My little love!" He swept her tightly against him, crushing her so that she couldn't breathe properly. "Don't you know that the reason I must have you is because you are the other half of myself?" Simon groaned.

Her senses swam as he swung her off her feet and headed toward the bedroom. He settled her with infinite gentleness in the middle of the huge bed in the darkened room and stood gazing down at her with such hunger and need flaring in the depths of his eyes that Kirsten reached out a hand to touch him reassuringly, letting her own expressive eyes mirror the love and need welling within herself.

Then, as if he could no longer wait for her, Simon was tugging off the damp jeans, slipping out of the shirt, and unfastening the hook's harness that wrapped around wide shoulders.

"Tonight," he told her deliberately, pulling back the covers, tucking her underneath, and sliding in beside her, "you'll have no doubts about your ability to satisfy your man. I could have told you from the beginning that the fires are inside you, waiting to burst into flame. But they must flame only for me, little one, only for me!"

Simon's hand reached out to wrap itself in her loosened hair, locking her head still for his kiss.

This was no gentle, exploratory caress. Kirsten was made to know all of his need and power and she felt herself instantly engulfed by it as he didn't seek permission to enter her mouth, but invaded it at once. Her only wish was to please, to satisfy, to give, as she let her emotions run free for the first time with a man. They leaped higher and higher in huge quantum jumps as Simon's hand stroked her whole body through the robe and nightgown from throat to hip, as if satisfying his sense of touch that she was really there beside him. Trembling beneath the strength of his hand, she reached out to explore his massive body, letting the tips of her fingers touch the masculine nipples, follow the line of his rib cage down to the tautness of his flat stomach and beyond.

His mouth broke free of hers with a wrench that left her gasping for air and descended to the hollow of her throat. Her eyes squeezed shut with pleasure as his lips trailed fire down to the edge of the nightgown and then his hand moved to go to work on the buttons of her robe. But now he didn't tease her by deliberately taking his time undoing them. Instead, with fingers that shook with need, he first fumbled with and then gently ripped the fragile material. In a moment she was free of it entirely.

"No more nightgowns or robes in bed, sweetheart," he muttered huskily against the softness of her breast. "I'll keep you warm enough!"

"Yes, Simon," she moaned in response to the heat of his mouth as it enclosed a hardened nipple. "Yes, Simon!" Her hand clenched convulsively around the tough muscle of his buttock and then relaxed to travel up the sinewy back, kneading and probing as it went.

"Touch me, Simon!" Hold me!" Kirsten was barely aware of her own breathless voice murmuring incoherently in the darkness, but Simon reacted to it as if it were another torch being added to his flaming, fiery desire.

"You're mine, little one. Tell me again! I want to hear you say it!" he ordered, moving one heavy thigh over her soft ones and letting the weight of his leg force its way between hers. Instantly Kirsten's moved apart to allow the further invasion. With each new caress, each new inch of her body explored, Simon was seeking more. He gave her no breathing space, no time to relax languidly beneath the waves of feeling, but demanded and pushed and took until she could do nothing else but respond to him in a series of ever deepening surrenders.

"I'm yours, Simon, my love," she whispered softly, wonderingly, feeling him stroke the sensitive inner part of her thighs. Higher and higher his hand moved until he knew beyond a shadow of a doubt of her readiness to receive him.

"So warm and moist and welcoming you are, sweetheart," he breathed. "I don't know how I ever waited until tonight to make you mine. I should have taken you to bed that first night!" His fingers moved in a delicate pattern to the center of her heated desire and Kirsten flinched in reaction.

"Simon!" she groaned. "Please, please touch me again!" she begged, arching herself against his hand, pleading for more of the strange sensation she had begun to sense would lead to some astounding place.

With a slashing, supremely masculine grin, Simon lifted his head to study her curious, expectant, wide-eyed look. His fingers moved again and he seemed to take great pleasure from the small tremor that shook her. She closed her eyes as a new, even higher level of need raced through her.

With a hungry growl, Simon rose briefly beside her and then settled himself firmly between her thighs.

"I can't wait any longer, honey," he warned, setting up shock waves that spread out to the tips of Kirsten's fingers.

For a stunned instant Kirsten gasped for air and then she felt him begin to move inside her as his hand sought her breast and his mouth covered hers. It was as if he would absorb her essence into his very being. Kirsten felt as if she were caught up in a huge, irresistible tidal wave that tossed her helplessly, gloriously about in its grip. The powerful, dizzying experience made her cling and cling and cling to the solid man above her who was at once the source of the storm and the only shelter.

Kirsten felt the tremors that Simon initiated begin to grow until they began to block out all other sensation. With a wondering, thrillingly excited sense of discovery, she felt them intensify, knowing only that Simon Kendrick was the amazing cause of all this, wanting to repay him completely in his own coin.

"I love you, I love you, I love you," she repeated over and over in a litany which found an echo in him.

"You're mine, forever, and I love you! God! How I love you!" Simon blazed fiercely, reaching down to lift her hips even more tightly against his.

And then the explosion came for Kirsten. It was all she had ever imagined it could be! A bursting, quaking, uncontrollable release that was made even more incredibly satisfying by the knowledge that Simon had gone over the thrilling edge with her! And then they were falling, falling . . .

It was a long time before Kirsten could bestir herself sufficiently to uncurl from the warmth of Simon's arms and look up into his face. When she did, she couldn't restrain a rueful grin at the look of sheer masculine contentment and satisfaction etched there.

"How does it feel to belong so completely to a pirate?" he asked with a rich chuckle.

"How did you know I thought of you like that?" Kirsten blinked, surprised. Was the man really a mind reader as he had once claimed?

"It was in your beautiful gray eyes so many times whenever you looked at me. I suppose the hook contributed toward the illusion? And the fact that I'd been a Marine?"

"I don't think it's an illusion!" Kirsten murmured. "You really are a pirate. But it's all right," she assured him seriously. "I always found Captain Hook much more exciting than Peter Pan!"

"You didn't answer my question," he reminded her, probing eyes searching her face.

"About belonging to you? It doesn't appear to be an intellectual decision. It's turning out to be one of those things a woman knows intuitively. But I warn you! I consider you as much my property as you consider me yours!"

"Good!" he announced with great satisfaction and kissed her soundly. "Then I suggest we toast our future. A future in which, no matter what happens, we will allow nothing to come between us!"

"What do you propose to toast this future with?"

"Silly girl," he grinned affectionately, pulling her close. "Come here and I'll show you!"

It was nearly four o'clock in the morning when Kirsten, hovering on the edge of sleep, mumbled, "I've just thought of something."

"Ummm?"

"What with one thing and another, I never heard the whole story of Hagood and his friend, Jensen. Was that what you called him?"

"I'll tell you all about it on the way to Coeur d'Alene," Simon promised and, hauling her against him, fell asleep.

When Kirsten opened her eyes to bright sunlight several hours later the heavy, comforting weight beside her was gone. She stretched, yawning widely, enjoying the sensation of wall-to-wall bed, and then waited. She didn't have to wait very long. Simon appeared in the doorway of the bedroom, a cup of steaming hot coffee cradled in his right hand.

"You've been very faithful to your promise of handling morning coffee," she laughed up at him as he towered beside the bed. She wondered how she could ever have thought she could go through life without having Simon about to wake up to in the mornings! She sat up to receive the saucer and then slid immediately back under the covers as she remembered that she didn't have a nightgown. It lay in a filmy, tattered pool beside the bed.

"Would you mind loaning me a pajama top or something, darling?" she asked politely.

"Don't own any," he informed her carelessly, dismissing the subject as he pushed the cup and saucer into her hand. He watched with amusement as she struggled to deal with the bedclothes and the coffee at the same time and then abruptly frowned, leaning forward to touch the side of her jaw.

"What the hell is this?" he demanded, fingering the bruised area gently.

Kirsten, lacking a free hand to raise to her face, smiled crookedly. "Is it starting to color badly?" she asked worriedly.

"Hagood hit you?" he growled.

"Well, I didn't exactly go along quietly," she explained. "What do you expect from the daughter of a Marine? There came a point during the struggle when the man apparently lost his patience with me."

"I'll kill him," Simon announced quietly and Kirsten, startled, believed him.

"Simon! Don't talk like that! I'm all right and Hagood is safely behind bars, isn't he? Let's just forget him! Please!" Kirsten was far too happy to waste time hating anyone this morning.

Simon stood still for a moment, considering, and then he shook his head slightly as if to clear it. "As long as he stays locked up and out of my sight, I'll let him be. But if he ever wanders back into our lives again, I'll definitely kill him."

Kirsten said nothing, knowing she would have to rely on the law and Hagood's own common sense to keep Simon from turning back into the cold-blooded warrior she had seen briefly last night.

"It's very late!" she said quickly. "What about work? Did you phone someone and tell them we're not going to be in today?"

"I told Silco that not only would neither of us not be in today, but that both of us were handing in our resignations at the end of the week!" Simon told her firmly. "You and I are going to make that vineyard support us from now on!" Period. The decision was made, Kirsten thought wryly.

"I picked up some things from your closet, and your contacts. I didn't realize you didn't have them in last night when I sent you home. Did you have any trouble driving?"

"Let's just say it's a good thing Richland rolls up the streets at night. There wasn't any other traffic on the road!"

Simon had downed his usual massive meal and was in the bathroom brushing his teeth when someone pounded on the apartment door. Kirsten set down the frying pan she had been drying and went to answer it before remembering that she wasn't in her own abode. She took in the smiling features of a pleasant-faced, dark-eyed man in his middle thirties and found herself returning the smile immediately.

"Rich Montgomery. You must be Kirsten?" he added, stepping into the room and extending one hand politely.

"Kirsten Mallory," she agreed, taking the hand. "Simon will be out in a minute, I'm sure. Won't you have a seat?" She examined their guest carefully. He grinned, catching her eye on him as he settled himself into one of the large, heavy chairs.

"Don't mind me," she told him cheerfully. "It's only that I've never seen a real, live government agent before! I've read so many novels . . ."

Rich Montgomery held up a hand, laughing. "Please, I'm not from the James Bond or Nick Carter school!" He glanced down at the neat suit he was wearing, which was doing its best to hide the slight paunch at his waistline. His figure together with his somewhat rounded face and happy eyes didn't go a long way toward making him look like a fictional undercover hero and his expression said he knew it.

"I wouldn't worry about it," Kirsten told him, knowing what he was thinking, "this is a much better disguise than if you wore an armory around under an evening jacket."

"Would you be dreadfully disappointed if I point out

182

that this isn't a disguise, that it's the real me, and that I spend most of my working hours shuffling paper?"

"Terribly. So don't tell me. Would you like a cup of coffee? Simon makes very good coffee, although it's a bit on the strong side."

"I've had it before," Rich told her wryly. "And that's putting it mildly. It's the classic horseshoe-floating variety. Yes, I'll have some, thanks. I've been up most of the night!"

"I'll be right out, Rich," Kirsten heard Simon call from the bedroom while she poured coffee.

"Before he gets here and monopolizes you, I've got some questions," she told Rich, hurrying back into the living room with the thick, dark brew. She thought fleetingly of seeing if something metallic would float on the surface and changed her mind.

"I'm not surprised. I haven't had a chance to fill Simon in completely. I tried to tell him what I could on the phone, but he wouldn't listen properly. Said something about calling from a police station and not wanting to hang around because he had things to take care of at home!"

"That sounds like Simon! The overbearing manager type. Knew it the minute I met him," Kirsten nodded equably.

"Actually, he can be very good at it." Rich smiled reminiscently, a dark memory flickering briefly in the pleasant eyes. "I and several others owe our lives to his 'management' technique!"

"Vietnam?" she asked softly, not wanting Simon to overhear. "I saw the Purple Heart he substituted in the shoebox. . . ."

"There's also a Navy Cross floating around somewhere," Rich told her gently.

Kirsten blinked. "Oh," was all she said, remembering the day she had come across the little case containing her father's Navy Cross from another war. "Awarded for extraordinary heroism in operations against an armed enemy." Kirsten shuddered.

"About Hagood . . ." she persisted carefully, not wanting Simon to know she had been talking about him.

"Yes, Hagood. And James Talbot. Are you certain you want to hear all the details, Kirsten?" Rich asked quietly.

"Yes, please."

"Well, as I tried to sketch out to Simon last night over the phone, Talbot and Hagood were partners in an interesting little enterprise, which had its economic base in the fact that it delivered certain very sophisticated electronics devices to governments that the United States has specified should not receive said devices."

"They were smugglers?" Kirsten asked, curious.

"On a very sophisticated level. There's quite a lucrative black market for high-level U.S. electronics. It's a field in which we still excel and there are countries willing to pay a lot of money for some of these items."

"But how? How did they get the stuff out of the country? How did they line up buyers?"

"Getting it out of the country was a very ingenious process. Were you aware, Kirsten, that James Talbot had spent some time as a mercenary after Vietnam?"

"No!"

"Well, he did. Primarily in Africa, as a matter of fact. He and Hagood went together and it was while they were there that they made the contacts they later sold to. There are a lot of nations seeking influence in Africa at the moment and it isn't all that difficult to contact them. Especially if you're in a quasi-military status as a mercenary is. In some of the countries the mercenaries come and go as near heroes. It's a minor problem for them to enter the country with whatever they wish and leave with a good deal of money."

"I see," Kirsten said rather blankly. "But Jim wasn't gone for very long periods of time. I mean, he disappeared, but not usually for more than a couple of days. How could he come and go that quickly?"

"Talbot had removed himself from the courier level of the operation. He ran the set-up. Hagood was his second-in-command. They simply lined up a few mercenaries who were open to a little extra adventure and a little extra cash. It wasn't hard to find interested men."

"And where do the lighter and the Purple Heart fit in?" Kirsten asked curiously, sipping her coffee.

"The lighter was the key. There was no fluid in it, you know. Just a tiny piece of microfilm rolled up inside." Rich Montgomery looked rather pleased with himself.

"I can't stand the suspense." Kirsten chuckled. "Please tell me what was on the film."

"The names of the foreign contacts and the codes used to reach them."

"Hagood didn't have his own copy?" Kirsten said, surprised.

"It would appear that James Talbot ran the show completely. He either didn't totally trust Hagood or didn't think he needed to know all the details. It would appear that Hagood had begun to resent his status. The authorities are rechecking the 'accident' Talbot had in his car."

"You think Hagood murdered Jim?" Kirsten whispered, unsettled by this new evidence of violence on the part of the man who had kidnapped her.

"It's a possibility. Talbot apparently told Hagood that if anything ever happened to him, he would make sure Hagood could carry on the operation."

"The letter to me from Jim, the one in the shoebox with the lighter and Heart. He seemed to think something might happen to him, but he certainly couldn't have suspected Hagood or he would never have left instructions for me to give Phil the stuff," Kirsten noted, thinking about the strange letter she had received the morning after her apartment had been searched.

Rich nodded. "It's largely conjecture at this point, Kirsten, but it seems Hagood 'manufactured' some trouble with one of the contacts. Enough to convince Talbot to hide for a couple of weeks and also do his duty by seeing to it that the crucial information needed to run the operation was protected in the event anything happened to him. Hagood apparently thought Talbot would see to it that the lighter came directly to him. He hadn't counted on Talbot's using you as a go-between. It took Hagood awhile to realize what had happened. He had already searched the house you and Talbot shared before he located you and performed the same exercise."

"The car," Kirsten mused, "the one I thought was following me the night I, uh, had trouble getting home from a date. It was the same dark blue as the one Hagood was using last night."

"Hagood was probably wondering just how much you knew at that point. He hadn't found the lighter and was deciding how to approach you about it."

"How did he even know the information he wanted was in the lighter?" Kirsten demanded.

"Because of this," Rich smiled, producing an envelope from his coat pocket and unfolding the short note inside. "It's a letter to Hagood from Talbot, probably written at the same time the shoebox was put in the mail to you."

"Telling Hagood to contact me for a few 'mementos' in the event anything happened, right?" Kirsten guessed.

"Near enough," Rich confirmed. "After reading this, Hagood knew what items had been left to him and guessed the lighter was the only one which could contain anything useful."

Montgomery broke off as Simon appeared, striding briskly into the room.

"Glad you could drop by, Rich. As you can see," he added cheerfully, tossing a set of keys in the air, "we're on our way out the door. Trust we'll see you again soon, pal. In the meantime, be sure and make a clean sweep of this Hagood affair! Come along, sweetheart," he ordered, walking toward the door and obviously expecting Kirsten to follow.

"Simon! What's gotten into you! I haven't had a chance to brush my teeth, and furthermore," she snapped waspishly, "I might remind you we have a guest!"

"She thinks she'll make a nagging wife yet, even though I keep telling her its hopeless!" Simon explained kindly to a grinning Rich. Then he looked over at Kirsten and chuckled. "Run along and brush your teeth, if you must. I'll give you two whole minutes to do it. Understand?" He turned back to Rich, ignoring Kirsten and giving her only

186

a large back to which she could direct her cutting remarks. She decided to brush her teeth instead.

Ten minutes later, having purposely taken more than the allotted two, Kirsten returned to the living room in time to see Simon putting into his coat pocket a strange object with a cord attached. It looked like the unusual weapon that had brought down Phil Hagood several hours earlier and it sent a chill down Kirsten's spine.

"You won't need it, you know," Rich Montgomery was saying quietly. "I've got Hagood and his friend Jensen sewed up very tight this time. You and Kirsten will be all right. I promise."

"I believe you, Rich. But the thing's a part of me now. I've carried it ever since that strange little man in Africa showed me how to use it. Last night was the first time I've ever had to put it to work, though, since those days."

"Do you ever hanker to get back into the business?" Rich asked very softly. "Harlan would give you your old job back at the drop of a hat." Neither man noticed Kirsten, who stood, frozen, in the hallway.

"Not in the least," Simon informed Rich quite readily, buttoning the pocket that held the little weapon. "I've known for a long time now that the only work I find truly satisfying is growing my grapes and making my wine. And when I met Kirsten, I knew she was the only other thing I needed in my life to fill it completely." He glanced over his shoulder, as if sensing her presence, and smiled at Kirsten.

"Ready, honey?" he asked easily. "We'll have to call your father and . . . Hey!" He laughed delightedly as Kirsten unstuck herself from the floor of the hall and practically flew across the room, hurling herself confidently into Simon's welcoming arms.

"I see your woman knows her place," Rich remarked, laughing, his dark eyes meeting Simon's over the top of Kirsten's head.

"Ummm," Simon agreed contentedly. "Right next to my heart!"